Content warning

This book contains disturbing materials that readers might find not to their liking.

I0545062

King's Heirs

Magical Academy

Lina Bengston

Published by Lina Bengston, 2021.

KING'S HEIRS

First edition. March 31, 2021.

Copyright © 2021 Lina Bengston.

ISBN: 978-1735549248

Written by Lina Bengston.

Table of Contents

Chapter 1

The day dragged on, but I filled the time by making a mental note of what I would need for our trip. I kept glancing at the clock as it inched its way slowly to three, until finally, the last bell rang, and I was the first one out the door and onto the waiting bus.

Even then, the bus couldn't get there soon enough. My legs bounced on the cold bucket seat as I stretched my neck to check if we were close. When I glimpsed the white trim of my house, I got up and rushed to the exit even before it came to a complete stop.

I had to refrain from racing to the front door. Until finally, I turned the knob and heard the familiar squeaking of the door from the ungreased hinges as I opened it. I discarded my backpack at the bottom of the stairs and sprinted to my opened suitcase that was sitting on top of my bed. I rummaged through the overflowing clothes as I went through the mental checklist I made in school and determined that everything was in order. Yeah, I might have gone a tad overboard since everything I own of value was inside the bag, but I wanted the trip to be perfect.

I'd planned every detail of this trip ever since Mom and I decided to go. My days off were spent in the library researching the city and my suitcase had been packed for a week. I must have taken it out at least three times to make sure I hadn't forgotten anything.

I took out the envelope that held all of my savings from my side drawer. I took out my last paycheck from my back pocket and tucked the whole thing inside the inner pocket of the suitcase. This had all of my college savings, any left over after helping Mom with the house bills went to my savings. However, over a week ago, my acceptance letter from the local college came in the mail and it shocked me to read that I had been offered a full scholarship. Mom and I couldn't contain our joy as we got the news. We clutched each other and had tears streaming down our faces as we jumped for joy. We had been busting our butts to save for college, but we still couldn't come close to our goal. Thank goodness the scholarship covered tuition, room, and board, which meant all of our savings were free for us to enjoy. It had been a relief to finally get a break from the harsh life we'd lived the past few years.

Mom and I stayed up all night discussing what we would do with the small pot of money we had saved up. I insisted she kept it to quit her second job, but Mom stubbornly argued that she loved her patients and enjoyed working.

Mom hadn't always had to work two jobs. When Dad was alive, she worked regular shifts and we even used to go on vacations. Our humble house was in a pleasant neighborhood, although it now showed the wear from the lack of upkeep since my dad's passing five years ago. He had insurance money, which went to pay his medical bills and for the funeral. The little money left, Mom kept in the bank for rainy days. With Mom stuck with the mortgage, bills and raising a teenage daughter alone, she had to get a second job to make ends meet.

I began working as soon as I turned fifteen to help her pay the bills and I also cleaned the house and served dinner after doing homework. This left me with little time for friends and parties, but I didn't mind since it was my way of giving back to my amazing mom.

Even though I was adopted, I felt loved by both my parents. They showered me with affection and support. Not once did I feel like I wasn't their own flesh and blood. Strangers couldn't even tell that we weren't related. Mom and I had light blond hair, hers slightly on the strawberry blond side, while mine was more on the white side. We shared the same petite features and the same five-five height while Dad had the same ocean blue eyes as mine.

My eyes trailed to the framed picture of the three of us sitting on my nightstand where Dad had a full smile, and his hands wrapped around Mom and me. "You're coming with us, Dad." I tucked it in the inside pocket of the suitcase so Dad could join us on the trip.

I checked the time. Mom wouldn't be off for a couple of hours. I double-checked our hotel reservations using the public library's Wi-Fi and I made sure my prepaid phone had full balance. I would only be reheating leftovers so the fridge would be empty when we left so I had nothing left to do.

I grabbed my backpack from the bottom of the stairs and pulled out my books so I could start on my schoolwork. Mom had spoken with my counselor and gotten me excused from school for the entire week. The teachers had handed my make-up work today, so I might as well start on it now so I could enjoy my vacation and time with Mom.

When my phone alarm buzzed, I quickly started reheating our dinner. I was clearing my books off the table when I heard the garage open and soon, Mom walked in looking exhausted but with a smile on her face.

"Smells good, honey." She kissed my head and dropped her stuff on the counter.

"Hi, Mom. How was work?"

"Oh, the usual. Nothing exciting."

"You can change. Dinner will be ready in a few minutes."

"Thanks, honey."

The microwave dinged, so I took out the chicken while the spaghetti still had a few minutes left in the oven. I made the salad, and after that, the oven beeped. I had served everything on the table by the time Mom came back in the room.

"I'm glad we have a lot of leftovers. I missed lunch today, so I'm starving."

I smiled as I scooped food on my plate. Mom always skipped meals when she worked. She had learned to pack a granola bar in her pocket and take quick bites when she was busy. She had such a good heart, and she never complained. My dad always scolded her and reminded her to take care of herself, but she always said her patients came first.

"I packed your bag but go through it and make sure I didn't miss anything," I said in between bites of meatballs.

"Thanks for thinking of everything. I really don't know what I would do without you." She reached over and squeezed my hand.

With a smile, I reached for the glass of water. It always made me uncomfortable when Mom said stuff like that since I felt the opposite—like a burden. If she hadn't adopted me, she wouldn't have had to work two jobs which I voiced out one night; however, she wouldn't hear of it. She insisted I was the best thing that happened to her and my father.

"So, do you know what you want to see first when we get there?" She chased a tomato with her fork and took a bite.

"Yes, I wanna see the three towers. I've never seen tall buildings. Do you think we can ride the elevators to the very top?"

"I don't think they're open to the public, but we can try the other, smaller buildings. We can pick the ones next to the towers so we can see them across from us."

I nodded and finished the rest of my plate. "I also want to cross the large bridge. Do you think we can stop and walk across, or can we only drive?"

"My friends from work said there's a spot where we can park and walk."

I flashed her a big smile as I got up and gathered my plate. "Go rest, Mom. We have a long drive tomorrow. I'll clean this up."

She kissed my temple and said, "Thank you, honey. Goodnight."

I wore a smile on my face as I washed the dishes and cleaned the kitchen. It would be impossible for me to sleep tonight. Tomorrow couldn't be here soon enough as I couldn't wait to see the city of San Divino. It was the largest and richest city in our country. There weren't many large metropolises around the world that could rival the city. It was known as the mecca of modern culture, as everything originated from San Divino. Everything cool happened in the city and the rest of us tried to emulate the city folks.

Pressing the power button on the TV, I flipped to the news channel. As usual, it was about San Divino. The anchor talked about the government's new regulations on residents of the city. It was ridiculous that they even had rules for the thousands of tourists that visited weekly. The city was always on the news—which made it more appealing for the tourists.

I couldn't imagine a city that size. Our small, sleepy town in Bry Ville had less than ten thousand people. Everyone knew everybody's business around here—we were all like an extended family—we didn't even have to lock our doors.

I forced myself to go to bed but tossed and turned for several hours. Anticipation buzzed inside me, and I couldn't settle down to sleep. I kept counting down the hours until we started our drive. I must have fallen asleep close to midnight.

I jerked awake as my alarm clock went off and quickly jumped out of bed with a big smile plastered on my face feeling energized, even though I had less than six hours of sleep. I rushed to get ready, and in less than thirty minutes, we'd loaded the car and secured the house—meaning the windows were shut and the doors were locked.

I sat in the front seat, giddy with excitement. Mom and I sipped our coffee cups quietly and ate our granola bars as we drove out of our sleepy town. I finally dozed off for a quick nap after three hours on the road.

"How much further?" I squinted and looked around the empty land.

"A couple more hours."

"Are you sure you don't want me to drive?"

"I'm fine, honey. I got plenty of sleep last night."

I turned the dial to my favorite station and music filled the car. Occasionally, I'd snap some selfies of Mom and me with the gorgeous scenery in the background. As we got closer, my veins filled with excited energy, until finally, I spotted a vast arch. My heart raced as I noticed the towering buildings just beyond the horizon. I craned my neck as we drove through and read a sign that said, *Welcome to San Divino.*

Mom and I flashed each other wide grins as we took in the slick and shiny cars of different makes and models filling up the four-lane freeway. At home we mostly had old cars and large trucks. The wide roads were intertwined with winding lanes of an overpass that extended next to buildings! I bet I could see inside the buildings when we drove by.

There was so much going on, I didn't know where to look. It felt as though we had entered another country. The towns we passed on our drive only had a few small buildings and some housing developments. However, this concrete jungle looked foreign with loud noises, fast cars and towering buildings—it was freaking amazing!

When we crossed the bridge, my nose was plastered onto the glass. We kept driving and at one point we stopped because of traffic and I could see over the bridge where small boats crossed the water. Mom kept driving—the metal bridge went on forever. It ended a few blocks before the edge of the city, closer to the water. There we found our small hotel nestled in between two glass buildings. We couldn't afford the exorbitant parking fees, so we found an alley and parked a few blocks down. We lugged our suitcase up the stairs and proceeded to the front desk.

The hotel looked old, but the beauty of it was still noticeable. It must have been a lovely boutique hotel back in the day, with faded golden trim and purple flowery wallpaper. The carpet had some holes in it, the corners of the wallpaper was peeling, and the fixtures were rusty, but it was clean and quaint and I still loved it.

My mom had requested the top room they had available for our booking, so we were on the seventh floor. *Seventh!* The tallest building in Bry Ville was four stories.

The room had two full-sized beds, and I took the one closest to the window.

"Oh my god, Mom. Look! We can see most of the city from up here."

"Oh, honey, this is gorgeous," she whispered. I snapped our picture, which had a beautiful view in the background.

We stood in front of the window for a few minutes, watching the lively city below us and if I squinted, I could see the marina to our right.

"I'm going to lie down for a bit," Mom said as she kissed my head.

I pulled the seat next to the window and watched the never-ending traffic, the business people, and the tourists bustling below.

As the sun crested the horizon, the blinding sunset made it challenging to watch below. So, I gathered the hotel brochures of tourist attractions and compared them to my research. Thank goodness the hotel had Wi-Fi, so I researched cheap options as Mom slept. I planned our itinerary for the next five days down to the hour.

Over the next few days, we walked all over town and crossed the entire bridge on foot. We did a lot of window shopping and visited different tall buildings. At the end of each day, we always made our way back to the marina. There was still so much to see, five days weren't enough to see everything. Mom and I were sad to be leaving the next day, but we were also grateful to have had this time together. The last four days were some of the best days of my life. I had had few of those since my dad passed, and so had Mom.

I kept snapping pictures of her carefree smile, which I hadn't seen on her in the last five years. "I'm so glad we took this trip, Mom." I lay my head on her shoulder as we walked hand in hand by the embarcadero. "Me too, honey. I missed this." She paused and looked over the ocean. I peeked at her and noted the sadness in her eyes as we watched the sunset. "I wish your father were here with us," she whispered after a few moments.

"Me too." I lay a hand on her shoulder, and silence engulfed us as we watched seagulls. The sun dipped lower and lower until only the top could be seen over the waterline. "You know, next year, when I move out, you don't need to keep the house and keep working two jobs. You can just enjoy life." I eyed her sideways.

Her eyes crinkled, and then her shoulders dropped. "I don't know, honey. That's the house your father and I had together. I'm not sure I can let go of it."

"I know, Mom. It's just, you're still young. He wouldn't want you to not live and enjoy life. When I'm not around, who will take care of you?"

"Where would you want me to live? I'm sure you wouldn't want me nearby."

"Of course I would. It would be cheaper for us to split a smaller house or an apartment. We could keep all the furniture and make it as similar as possible. Especially Dad's corner. We'll keep his chair and his side table and his posters in the living room."

Her face brightened up, and she asked, "Are you sure?"

"Yes, Mom."

"I love you, honey. I'm so lucky to have you."

"I love you too, Mom. I'm the lucky one."

We stayed until the sun completely disappeared, and then we caught the trolley back to our hotel. We hadn't realized how late it was, so by the time it dropped us off, it was utterly dark, and the streets were empty.

"Wait, did we get off at the wrong stop?" Mom asked as we looked around the empty streets.

"I don't know. It looks different at night." We didn't venture far from our hotel at night and we always stayed where there were people and restaurants around. However, this place was dark and deserted.

"The water is that way, and I see the enormous tower behind us. Let's walk in that direction," Mom said as she tugged on my hand. We walked towards the tall tower, hoping it would guide us back to our hotel.

We had been out bright and early on our first day and walked inside the white tower close to our hotel. Security quickly told us that the building wasn't open to the public. Needless to say, I was so bummed because each of the towers had a hundred and fifty floors. However, security pointed us to the next tallest building accessible to the public and we were able to go up to the one hundred and tenth floor using the elevators, and then we climbed the stairs to the rooftop. I remembered being left speechless as I looked down on the city. The wind whipped through my hair as I closed my eyes and stretched out my arms—it felt like I was flying. The tower was across from us and I couldn't imagine how it would feel being on the very top.

There are three towers and each could be seen from half the city. Depending on which section of the city you were in, you'd be able to spot a tower, each lit with different colors. The one behind our hotel was white. So, we kept an eye on it as we walked towards it. We walked for several blocks until we reached a dead end. We each looked around for an alternative but there was no other choice but to cross a dark alley. Mom and I eyed each other warily and with no words needed, we clutched each other's hands tightly and entered the dark alley.

The hairs on the back of my neck prickled, and cold flooded my spine. Soon I was tugging my mom's hand as we sprinted through. Then, I heard heavy footsteps behind us as we ran.

With the light at the end of the alley in sight, we took longer and faster strides. My eyes were trained to the light which was only footsteps away from what felt like our freedom. I tugged at Mom's hand, but she was roughly yanked away from me. I heard her intake of breath and then her scream—which was cut off suddenly.

"Mom!" I turned and saw a man with long scraggly hair holding Mom against his chest. Her feet were flailing with only one shoe on. She had a white-knuckle grip on the man's arm as she tried to force him away from her, but it was useless against his strength.

"Let go of her!" I yelled as I stepped forward which made his head snap up, but I froze and my eyes grew in fear as red deadly eyes stared back at me. Long fangs protruded over his lips dripping with blood—Mom's blood.

Mom hung limp like a rag doll, her shirt dark with blood. She was no longer fighting. My face filled with heat, and my vision narrowed at the man who held my mother as she bled to death. Adrenalin kicked in, and I shrieked and lunged at the man. However, I never made contact. Instead, I hit the concrete that burned my elbows as I hadn't gotten a chance to brace for my fall.

I looked up and saw a large animal latch its massive jaws around the man's shoulder. He let go of my mom and her body fell, twisted at a weird angle.

I crawled to her and pulled her to my lap. The large gash on her neck still poured blood, so I covered it with my hands. "Mom, you're going to be okay. Help! Please help! Mom, look at me." I looked around frantically, but no one was around. The man and the wolf were at the other end of the alley now. With one hand, I pulled my phone out and dialed, but there was no service, so I tried Mom's phone, but it was the same. "Mom, please wake up!" I sobbed.

Her eyes fluttered, and blood gushed out of her mouth. She lifted her hand and barely touched my cheek, then it fell heavily at her side. "Mom, Mom! Please. No. Stay with me."

She opened her eyes, and for the first time, she gazed at me clearly. With a choked voice, she said said, "I... lov..." She took in a raspy breath and more blood poured out of her mouth.

"Mom. Mom! I love you too! Please stay with me. Please. I can't... Please!" I screamed, pleaded and sobbed. But she didn't move. I rocked her body and knew she was gone. There was a kind of flaccidity to her body that wasn't there before—something about dead bodies felt different; it didn't feel the same as someone sleeping or someone who fainted.

However, she still felt warm, so she might still wake up. "Help! Help!" I screamed until my voice was hoarse, but no one came.

Chapter 2

"She's gone."

I twisted and saw a large, bearded man standing behind me.

"You need to come with me. There will be more of them."

I tightened my hold around Mom. "I'm not leaving my mom."

"I will have her body moved, but we need to go." He stepped closer and extended his hand towards me.

A sob broke out as I frantically shook my head, then I threw myself on her chest as I wailed. I didn't care if her blood got all over me. I couldn't let go. *She had to come back.*

I felt the man's hand on my arm, and a jolt of shock hit me. I flinched as my gaze snapped into his face.

His eyes turned into yellow slits—animal-like. I froze in fear, but I couldn't let go of my mom's body, so I scrambled backward, dragging her with me. "What are you?" My eyes darted up and down the dark alley, seeking a way to get away from this creature.

"I think you know, but the question is, why don't I know you?"

"What...what are you talking about?" I kept my mom's body covered with mine.

We heard distinct footsteps at the end of the alley and both our heads turned at the sound.

"We need to go," he said in a hurried tone. I squinted at the dark alley and remembered the man with red eyes and figured I was safer with this man. "I'm not leaving my mom," I stated firmly.

"Fine." He lifted my mother's body like it weighed nothing.

My eyes grew, and I froze mid-step. "Where are you taking us?"

"Just follow me. Hurry." Something about his tone made me follow, so we rushed out of the alley into a large, tinted SUV parked on the street. He gestured for me to open the back door where he laid my mother gently on the back seat.

I eyed the pristine upholstery as Mom's blood seeped into the luxury car, but he didn't seem bothered by it. Soon we were speeding down the road, then we entered the white tower's parking garage. *Who was this man, and what was with his eyes? He has to be someone important if he could just drive into the tower.* The guard said that the building was a private property, mostly used as a residence.

He kept driving up until we were at the very top, then we had to go through another gate. As soon as he entered, my eyes grew in surprise as the place morphed into a private garage rather than a building parking lot. It was a large open space with black tiles and white walls. He parked the large SUV next to other luxury cars. *No wonder the stain didn't bother him—he had a dozen other cars.*

We stayed in the car for a few moments in awkward silence until finally, he turned to me. "I will have my men take care of the body and have it buried at a private cemetery nearby. We can have my men fetch your things and take care of anything you need back home."

The mention of my mom's body had my brain going blank. I breathed through the tightness in my chest and nodded my head numbly—past caring who this mysterious man was.

This nightmare needs to be over; I can't even register the bizarre events that had happened tonight, let alone think about back home. I just want Mom back. Crawling over the hump of the center console, I threw myself at Mom's stiff body. Her cold and rigid body made me flinch and caused my chest to tighten and feel like it was caving in. I struggled to take deep breaths as I called for Mom to come back, I kept calling to her until my voice was hoarse. I barely felt the man pull me off my mom as he half carried me inside.

No longer aware of my surroundings, all I could do was cry. I couldn't stop. I kept going until I had no more tears to shed. I kept thumping my chest since it ached so bad. I wanted to rip it out of me and join my mom, together we could see Dad. I lay motionless until the tightness in my chest eased, and I found I could breathe again.

It must be close to dawn since the sky looked light. I was in a large room with dark furniture, laying on an opulent bed. The man leaned against the door frame with a blank look on his face.

I sat up and lifted my shirt to wipe my face but dropped it as it was crusted with dried blood. "Where am I?"

"You're at my home. I just wanted to make sure you were okay. There are some clean clothes in the bathroom. When you're done cleaning up, join me outside so we can chat." Without waiting for an answer, he closed the door.

The massive room was larger than our living room and kitchen combined. I sat frozen for a few moments, I sucked in a stuttered breath, then padded my way into the bathroom and stripped off my sticky clothes. The hot shower washed away the blood and tears as I scrubbed my skin raw, I didn't leave until the water ran clean. I leaned my head on the tile and had to take deep breaths as my chest felt like it was splitting in half. I wanted the shower to drown me and take my pain away but instead, I wrapped myself in a large, plush towel and noticed that the small seating area had a stack of brand-new clothes which fit perfectly. I dressed robotically, not caring what I had on, just noticing how soft the fabric was.

I avoided the bed since it had blood stains on it and I no longer want to see my mom's blood. So, I stepped out of the room; my brows rose and for a moment I stood in the middle of a massive hallway with opulent trimming and life-size paintings, unsure of where to go. I slowly made my way down the hall passing several doors, wondering where I should go. With hesitation, I kept wandering until I heard soft music playing. I had to pause a few times with a tilt of my head as I tracked the sound. Finally, I found the giant man with his hair tied behind his back in a short ponytail, sitting behind a grand piano playing a sad melody. His fingers gracefully glided across the keys as his muscular arms strained against his white shirt. He was an imposing man, but he wore a gentle expression as he played the song that matched my loss.

The music stopped, and his grey eyes met mine.

"Please don't stop on my account." I said as I stood awkwardly by the threshold.

"No, I was just killing time. Please have a seat." He gestured at the white leather sectional. My eyes traveled around the pristine, wide-open space surrounded by glass, but the view distracted me. I stepped closer to the glass wall and my eyes grew as I saw the little dots of the city lights. I traced the coastline and saw a portion of the bridge.

"The view is even better from the rooftop," he said as he followed my gaze.

"Can you see the entire city from up here?"

"No, just my territory."

My head snapped in his direction, and I frowned at his response.

He studied me for a minute, then said with his brows drawn together, "I see your confusion and I don't smell any lies on you, but you can't be a newly made wolf. Otherwise, you wouldn't have alpha blood." He scratched his neatly trimmed beard as he watched me closely. "Who are you?"

"What are you talking about?" My frown got deeper as his words registered in my foggy brain. "You mean, that's what you are? Your eyes. The animal in the alley," I mumbled, my gaze shifting to the floor, as I pictured the animal in the alley. "You saved my life, didn't you?" I looked up, gauging his reaction.

"You mean to tell me you don't know what you are?" He turned entirely toward me. His forehead wrinkled. "That's not possible. You have alpha blood. It's impossible not to shift."

My emotions were frayed, and I had very little patience. "What is 'alpha,' and why do you keep insisting that I have it?" I snapped in irritation.

He squared his shoulders as he stood taller while his gaze kept me captive. I felt something inside me stir—something foreign, as I stared back at the giant man. His kind demeanor was long gone; before me was a predator. His eyes were sharper and his features stern. I stood before the shadow of the beast

I had seen in the alley. Frozen in his gaze and unable to look away, something inside me knew it meant life or death for me if I shifted my gaze away, but I couldn't look away even if I wanted to.

"Are you challenging me?" he growled, baring his teeth as his eyes turned yellow once more.

Something in me awoke. My skin crawled and it felt like I needed to shed it. Like it was getting too tight, and it didn't fit me, but I still didn't break my gaze away from the yellow eyes and the soft growls of the man in front of me. My body temperature increased, which made me feel feverish until the heat intensified, and I felt like my skin would melt away. It reached a point I could no longer stand, so I opened my mouth to scream. Instead, an animalistic snarl escaped from me as I dropped on all fours. My vision changed—everything looked sharper, and the unfamiliar scents surrounding me distracted me.

I sensed a threat, and a giant black wolf stood in place of the man. Fear flooded my veins, and the instinct to protect myself filled me. I faced the beast entirely, and I opened my mouth to speak, but my voice wouldn't come out. Instead, I heard a bark. *What the fuck!* I looked down and saw paws instead of my feet. I lifted my paw in front of my face and noticed the tip of my nose. I ran and felt a tail whip my side, so I chased it in circles and finally saw that it was my tail. *I'd turned into a fucking animal. What the fuck happened to me?*

I ran around the room, knocking things over, terrified. I couldn't find the exit, so I hid behind the couch and tried crawling underneath it, but I couldn't fit.

"You weren't lying. Is this the first time you've shifted?"

I looked up from behind my paws. *Yes, I had fucking paws.* They uncovered my eyes and I saw the man's head peeking from the sofa. "Shift back so we can talk."

How the fuck do I do that? I looked at my paws, and then I conveyed everything I could with my eyes.

"Oh, that's right. You've never done this before. Let's see. This should be second nature to all Shifters. It's the same as shifting into a wolf. It should come naturally. You just think about your human form and you should be able to shift back."

I eyed him skeptically. *What did I have to lose?* So, I closed my eyes and did as he instructed.

"Oh, also, you need to think about your human form with the clothes you were wearing, or you will shift back naked. You can't manifest clothes you weren't wearing before you shifted."

I glared at him and rolled my eyes. *Yeah, like it was that easy. Now I had to worry about being naked! What the fuck had I been wearing?*

I didn't remember what I wore, but I remembered how it felt. With the feeling in mind, I also pictured what I saw in the mirror as I brushed my long blond hair; then pictured my small nose, pointy chin, and non-existent lips. Soon, heat filled me, but instead of waiting for it to get overwhelming, I released it. When I opened my eyes, I was me again.

"Thank fuck!" I patted my chest, "I thought I would be stuck as an animal forever." I inspected my arms and hugged my body, then dropped on the couch with a sigh. "What the hell was that?"

With a curious look, he said, "I also would like to know the answer to that question."

"Can you at least tell me what you are?"

"You mean you know nothing of this world?" He said as he sat on the other seat.

I shook my head. "My mom and I are...were...she...I'm from Bry Ville. This is the first time I've been to the city."

His eyes widened. "This is even more unusual than I thought." He was quiet for a moment, with a look of deep contemplation. "You've been through enough, so let me try to explain it as succinctly as possible." He got up and gestured for me to join him. He led me to another room, where a feast was laid out on a long table. I eyed the room in confusion. *Was he expecting more people?*

"Have a seat. You will soon find out that after you shift, you need to replenish the calories you lost, so Shifters eat more than the average human." He filled his plate as he spoke.

I grabbed small helpings of foreign food and took a bite of the dinner roll. I had little appetite, but I felt weak. So, I forced myself to eat.

"First, let me introduce myself. My name is Rahl Fier. I'm the king of the Shifters."

My fork froze close to my mouth as my eyes grew in surprise. "King? Shifters?" I dropped the utensil and studied him closely. He looked normal, aside from turning into an animal. *Then again, didn't I do that just a few minutes ago? I must have hit my head or something.*

He chuckled. "It's refreshing having someone treat me like a normal person. Yes, San Divino is the home of the supernaturals. There are three types: the Shifters, Vampires, and the Casters—they're magic wielders."

My throat tightened up. "You mean, the man in the alley. The one that..."

"Yes. A rogue Vampire murdered your mother. It's against the rules for any of us to hurt humans. The government has been keeping a close eye on us to make sure we follow the rules and granted us little freedom when the three supernatural rulers guaranteed that the humans would be safe. This incident is a nightmare. I'll need to meet with the Vampire King and Queen and discuss their rogue problem. However, before I do that, I need to make sure you're safe."

"What do you mean?"

"I wanted to make sure that tonight was a random attack and not targeted."

"You mean me?" I pushed my plate away and leaned back. "My mother was killed because of who I am?"

"No. Vampires wouldn't want to attack a Shifter. That would mean war."

A loud breath escaped me; I didn't think I could live with the thought that I had caused her death. "So, each tower is owned by the ruling supernatural?"

"Yes. White is for the Shifters, and the surrounding areas are my territory. The red are Vampires, and the blue is for the Casters—witches and wizards."

"When you say Shifters, you mean more than wolves?"

"Yes. There are different Shifter clans. They all answer to me. As their alpha King, they are connected to me. Even the ones that don't live in the city. That's why I find it unusual for you to exist without me knowing. Especially since you're an alpha."

"You keep saying that. What does it mean?"

"Every Shifter has the potential to lead, but to lead the whole Shifter race, you need to be an alpha—a dominant.

Usually, alphas are only bred from the royal line. Sometimes a dominant is born from a non-royal line because an alpha is still an alpha, royal or not. Over the past few centuries, there have been fewer and fewer wolves born because there have been fewer wolf alphas."

"Are wolves always alphas?"

"After the dragon Shifters, who are no longer around, the wolves are the next strongest Shifters. Wolves have ruled the Shifters for as long as I can remember. Although the other Shifter clans outnumber the wolves, we are still dominant." He took a sip from his wineglass and studied me.

"What's even rarer is a female alpha wolf. If our community would have known about you, we would have cherished you. We would have kept you here, safe, since our species depends on it."

Fear built in my belly.

"I'm sorry. I didn't mean to scare you. I would never hold you against your will. I'm just saying that you're a mystery—an impossibility."

"Why?"

"First, you shouldn't have been able to go this long without shifting. Second, like I said, all Shifters are connected to me, so I know every single one of my people. I would have known about you the moment you were born."

"I was adopted," I whispered.

"How old are you?"

"Eighteen."

"What's your name?"

"Viola Price."

He shook his head. "You shouldn't exist," he mumbled.

No kidding. I should be with my parents.

"I'm sorry. I was just thinking out loud. I didn't mean to be insensitive."

"What happens to me now?"

"I think you should stay here until you can get a better handle on your new abilities."

My eyes prickled. "Where's my mom?"

"They are preparing her body. I will bring you to her when it's time."

I sat quietly as I played with my food. *I'd had enough for today.*

"Viola, you may be excused if you want to head back to your room," he said gently.

I nodded my thanks and got up, numb from the events of the day. My mind was shutting down, and I could no longer process any of this.

I found my way back to the room and laid in bed, wide awake for hours without moving, feeling or thinking. I just existed. *Maybe I'd wake up from this nightmare tomorrow, and everything would go back to the way it was.* My throat tightened up, and I choked on a sob. I took a deep breath and stopped it before it began. I closed my eyes and got back to the place where I just existed. Eventually, I fell asleep.

MY EYES WERE SWOLLEN, and I had trouble opening them entirely when I woke up. However, I laid in bed, waiting and not wanting to move. For a moment, I felt peace. A part of me still had hope, and I wasn't filled with pain. It had been hours, and I'd stayed in the same position, ignoring my growling stomach and my bodily needs. I even dismissed the knock on the door. Eventually, they all went away, and I fell asleep again. This was where I needed to be—No pain.

I JERKED AWAKE BECAUSE of someone's presence in the room.

"I've given you three days to mourn. You barely touched the food I had sent in, and you haven't changed out of your clothes," Rahl said.

I turned away from him, as tears fell down my cheeks.

"Look, Viola, we can no longer delay your mother's funeral. You need to go see her today, or she is getting buried without you."

My head snapped in his direction.

He laid a bag at the corner of the bed. "Those were on her. Your belongings from the hotel are in the closet, along with something appropriate to wear to the funeral. Come find me when you're ready." He patted my leg and left the room.

My tears ran freely now as I pulled the bag closer. In it were Mom's ring, necklace, cellphone, and wallet.

I heaved a stuttered breath in as I unclasped the necklace and threaded her ring, as a pendant joining my dad's ring that she always wore around her neck. I turned her phone on and scrolled through her messages. Her friends and work called frantically at first, then just her close friends sent grief and shocked messages. I didn't read further. I couldn't handle other's grief when I was barely holding my own. I checked her email, but it was the same thing. There was some other business stuff that I skipped. Then I scrolled through her pictures, and for the first time in days, my lips turned up into a smile. On the phone were pictures of Mom on her last day, the two of us, happy. I kept scrolling through her photos, and although tears ran down my face, they didn't feel like my chest would split open. It felt cleansing, I was able to function around the pain.

After a few hours, I mechanically got ready and sought the King. I needed to see my mom.

AFTER ONLY A FEW MINUTES in the car, Rahl drove past double gates into a nearby cemetery. We walked into a white, cold building and on the dias was my mother. She laid on a slab wearing a white dress and a white strip of fabric wrapped around her neck. She looked like an angel. I stepped closer and raised a shaking hand, but I paused and looked up at Rahl in question.

He nodded to state that it was okay to touch her.

I laid my hand slowly over hers and flinched as the cold reminded me of the night I felt her rigid body. My chest tightened and the dam of tears exploded out of me. I threw myself at her and wailed. "Mommy, why did you leave me? Please take me with you. I can't go on without you. Please. Mom. Please," I bawled. My chest heaved painfully as I cried like a child, Not caring that there were people around me. I begged and pleaded but the soul-shattering sobs didn't bring my mother back.

I briefly noted that Rahl rubbed my back in quiet support. He didn't interrupt, he just stayed with me until I was out of tears. Eventually, I allowed them to take my mother to get cremated as Rahl held me as I lost it over and over. When I was steady on my feet, he led me outside where we sat in the car. I must have dozed off again since I felt a gentle tap on my shoulder. "Viola."

I raised my eyebrows and he hesitantly handed me my mother's ashes.

I clutched the cold, dark vase and sat in silence for a few moments.

"Do you know what you want to do with the ashes?"

I nodded, then swallowed the tight lump in my throat. "She would want to be scattered somewhere. It was what we did with my dad."

I fingered a pendant that was wrapped around the urn absentmindedly.

"That is something you can wear. It has some of her ashes in it."

My chest tightened, and my shaky hands unlatched the chain. Rahl helped me place the necklace next to my mom's necklace. Mom never took off her necklace, now it was my turn to wear their rings around my neck. I clutched the pendant and the rings and a part of me felt better—my mom and dad will always be with me.

"Thank you," I whispered.

He nodded.

"I think she would want to be scattered by the ocean. She was happy there."

He backed out of the parking lot. I leaned my head back and watched the city pass by, then we drove into a private entrance in the marina. Needing to take occasional deep breaths, I quietly followed as we boarded a large ship. I gazed out the water as we sailed a few miles away from the city. Mom would have liked this. My mom's smile as she gazed out at the marina flashed and I thought of the moments we had shared throughout the years and silly fights we'd had. I remembered when we lost Dad, she cried at night and I could hear her through her bedroom door but when she's with me she stayed strong. Not once did she show any weakness, even if she struggled, she still found a way to fight and be kind. I knew she missed Dad every day, but it didn't stop her from being a great mother. *Now they can finally be together. She can finally rest. I love you Mom. Please say hi to Dad for me.*

I smiled and nodded to Rahl. *I was ready.* He stepped away as I said a prayer and cried some more. When I finally scattered Mom's ashes, I watched as the wind blew her ashes away. With a deep breath, I said goodbye to my mother, my old life, and my old self.

I was ready to face my new reality.

Chapter 3

"What?" I must have misheard him, so I stared at Rahl with a furrowed brow while my fork hovered over my untouched plate.

"You need to go to Magnus Academy. We have exhausted all possibilities, but we still don't know where you came from," Rahl said in between bites of baked chicken and vegetables.

"You're sending me away?" My face twisted into a frown.

"Of course not. You know that's not the case," he said in a solemn voice with his eye trained on me, forgetting about his dinner.

Rahl had graciously taken me in and taken care of me since he found me in the alley. I'd lived with him for almost six months now, and I had no interest in returning to my old life—alone. Not even the prospect of college was enough to make me go back so I had to turn down my scholarship. He had been a gracious host and the only thing he demanded was I finished high school. Therefore, I grudgingly did all the work assigned by my old school and earned a diploma.

I moodily pushed the food around my plate without taking a bite. Finally, I met Rahl's eyes. "I don't need to learn anything. I have you." I pleaded as the heavy feeling in the pit of my stomach grew, and my eyes burned from unshed tears.

"Viola, you'll do fine. You're a wolf alpha." He waved his knife and continued to slice the chicken.

"I know nothing about being a wolf or the supernaturals. I'm not ready." I stabbed at the chicken as if it was the reason for my predicament.

Rahl tirelessly hunted down the Vampire responsible for my mom's attack and found him shortly after the funeral. I heard the Vampire king himself doled out the punishment, which I begged to attend, but Rahl wouldn't hear of it. He wanted me as far away as possible from the Vampires. After I heard that the monster was gone, I slept all night, and my nightmares subsided.

After that, I focused all of my energy in unraveling the mystery of my past. The obsession with finding out my past had grown in the last couple of months. However, we had no luck in finding my biological parents. Even my adoption papers turned out to be a dud. My birth parents' names were fake, which made sense since I wasn't human. Rahl said I couldn't have alpha genes if I were half-human. I'd been too consumed with research that I hadn't paid much attention to Rahl when he tried to teach me how to be a proper Shifter.

"You'll be fine. Plus, my heirs will be there."

I raised an eyebrow. "Your heir? I didn't know you had an heir." I took a bite of the tip of the asparagus and chewed slowly.

"Yeah. I have two. They'll be with you at the academy. They came for a brief visit twice, but you've been mourning." His grey eyes softened as he looked at me.

I'd spent the first few weeks in bed, hardly eating, hoping to be reunited with my parents. In the beginning, it felt like I was close to seeing them once again. Eventually, Rahl mandated I join him at dinner, which I hated at first, but ultimately, it was something I started looking forward to. We'd gotten closer. I really enjoyed his company. He was like a close uncle I had grown attached to. I don't know how I would have survived without his support. He even took care of the needed paperwork to sell my house and other insurance stuff I knew nothing about. He'd also been patient with me and allowed me to mourn on my own time. He never pushed me or demanded anything from me.

It took me months before I could walk inside my old house, but I felt better once I packed everything up and sold everything. I kept a few items I couldn't part with, which now lived in my room at Rahl's tower. With the house's sale and my mom's savings, I gained a small fortune to my name. Also, Rahl refused to take rent money and paid for everything.

"I don't want to leave, I'm not ready."

He reached for my hand and squeezed it. "You're tough. I've seen it. I know you'll do well in school. Plus, it's required for all alphas. I've been putting it off for as long as possible, but the semester is starting, and you turned down your college acceptance. There's no other choice."

I stared at him, racking my brain for a good counter argument but came up blank. Instead, a small part of me wanted to learn more about my powers. If only I knew how to use my powers, then I could have protected Mom. I vowed to myself that never again would I be a victim or watch anyone I love suffer. Rahl had me go through some random tests but he couldn't figure out why I was so different from other Shifters so he couldn't really teach me fully how to unlock my true potential.

"I'll still be here if you need me. This is your home now. You can come back during breaks. My heirs hardly visit, but I'm sure I'll see you during your breaks." His warm smile rose upon his face.

His assurance eased my worry. He was the only family I had left and I didn't want to lose him. "Fine. I'll give it a shot."

"Thank you. Plus, I have a feeling you'll uncover your past there. Everyone attends the university. I'm certain someone knows something about your biological parents."

"You think so?" I pushed my plate away and dabbed my mouth with the napkin.

He raised his eyebrows and looked pointedly at my half-full plate.

I shrugged. My lack of appetite had been a constant argument. He always pushed me to eat. He worried that I ate very little for a Shifter. It had also baffled him why I hardly shifted. He said it was uncommon for me not to change at all. Aside from the night at the alley, I only turned when he'd forced it out of me a handful of times.

"Yes. There might be more to your past that we don't know. Meanwhile, I'll continue to search here."

"Thank you, Rahl. I don't know how I would have survived if I didn't have you."

He looked taken aback, and then his face split into a smile. "You're welcome, Viola." His eyes filled with tenderness. Then he grinned and pushed a bowl of pudding in front of me.

I rolled my eyes but picked up a spoon.

"When do I leave?"

"Tomorrow."

My eyes grew. "That soon?"

He shrugged, avoiding my eyes. "I really didn't know how you would take it. I must admit, I'm surprised at how well you're handling it."

I sighed. "You're right. I can't hide here forever. I also want to know about my past. I need to find direction and learn more about my powers. Even though I want to stay here and pester you forever." I grinned.

"You are welcome to stay here forever, Viola. I just want you to acclimate into our world."

I flashed him a smile and nodded, then finished the bowl of yumminess.

He grinned at my empty bowl. "I will see you off tomorrow, but Jim will drive you. Call me anytime you need anything. I will have Martha pack what you'll need. Everything is all sorted out with the dean. Just pack anything specific you want to take with you."

We finished our dinner and spent the rest of the time enjoying our last night together.

"YOUR STUFF IS IN YOUR room, Viola. You take care of yourself. Call us if you need anything," Jim, Rahl's second-in-command, said as he released me from his warm embrace. I'd gotten close to him as well, even though he wasn't around as often. He was like an older cousin who was super sweet and funny.

"Thanks, Jim. I'll miss y'all. Tell everyone I'll be back to visit, and thanks for everything."

"Sure thing, kiddo." He waved and walked out the door. I watched him for a moment before making my way back to the leather couch. The stuffy room with a dome ceiling and grand chandelier was where the receptionist told me to wait until the dean was ready to see me. With my arms crossed, my leg tapped the polished wooden floor to hide my anxiety.

The moment Jim pulled up to the gates of the academy, I already knew I wouldn't like it. The grand arch entrance with carved statues and lush green grass looked too strict for my taste. The building itself was castle-like, a typical snobby elite university that most likely housed many uptight and boring students.

A country girl like me didn't belong in a place like this. I didn't do well with structure and rigid rules. I followed Jim quietly with lead in my stomach, but when I noticed the students wearing uniforms, I had to talk myself into not doing anything drastic, like hiding in the car's trunk or something.

The heaviness in my stomach grew as we ventured further into the school. By the time we made it to the dean's office, I had lost my ability to speak. Jim and I had stopped in front of the lady with a large oak desk as I contemplated how to convince Rahl to let me go back and stay with him.

She directed Jim and me to wait on the couch, which had been over thirty minutes ago.

Maybe I could call Rahl and tell him that this was a mistake. I glanced at the lady, seeing if she'd be able to hear me if I made a phone call. Then, glancing down at my phone, I decided to just text. I was scrolling through the names when I heard footsteps approach. I looked up to a short, balding man wearing a big smile.

"I apologize for the wait, Ms. Price. There was an urgent matter I had to deal with that came up last minute. Please come with me."

I pocketed my phone hesitantly and followed him with a sigh. We passed large wooden double doors and went straight to an enormous mahogany desk with intricate details that sat in the middle of the room. Then he directed me to sit in front of the desk as he took his seat. Across the room were cozy couches by the fireplace, and the walls were lined with rows and rows of thick, ancient texts. My eyes darted back to the soft cushions of the sofa. He must reserve the couch for friends or more casual visits.

I looked back at him and noticed him eyeing me with a slight cock of his head. He didn't shift his gaze, which made me uncomfortable. I moved my weight from the firm, leather chair and sat up straighter with raised eyebrows.

He cleared his throat and said, "I'm sorry, Ms. Price."

"You can call me Viola."

"Viola. I apologize for staring. I didn't mean to make you uncomfortable. There's just something unusual about your energy. Something I haven't felt before."

What the...? "What does that mean?" I twisted my hands together to keep my anxiety in check. I didn't think I could handle any more surprises.

"I don't know, dear. I can sense the alpha in you, but it isn't like the other alphas. I also can sense something else, something more dominant. As I said, it's not something I've felt in the past."

"Rahl didn't say anything was different about my energy," I mumbled.

"Yes. The king has been in touch, and he mentioned your unusual circumstance. He asked me to help unearth your past. Once again, I must apologize. I know this is all new to you. So, let me start by telling you a little about our school. This academy houses all three types of supernaturals before they join the adult community. Usually, students come here right after they study with humans for their first sixteen years of life. The royals deemed it necessary for everyone to learn how to be around humans and learn basic human studies. Then they come here and spend the next four years honing their powers. Afterward, they move on to specialize. They focus on a specific talent and gear their studies to what they plan on doing as an adult. You will join the specialty students."

I nodded.

"Just like the city, there are three towers—one for each species. Depending on the classes you are taking, it can either be species-oriented or mixed. For example, shifting studies are specific to Shifters, so you will only have Shifter students. Casting studies will only have wizards and witches. In combat strategies, which are mandatory for all students, you will have all species combined. It's important to the royals for all the species to get along, so they wanted to have several classes that allow interspecies interactions. The cafeteria is a common area along with the library, gym, and quad. Are you following me so far?"

I jerked my head even though my insides had gone cold when he said I would be in the same room as Vampires. I didn't know how I would react if I ever saw one.

"Now, as your dean, I meet incoming students and assess each talent. It helps with class placement. Since you're unfamiliar with our world, I will run down some essential pieces of information. Shifters are known for their senses, while Vampires are known for their speed. Vampires and Shifters are equal in their strength. Casters cast spells and manipulate the surrounding energy. Usually, a Caster is skilled with only one type of energy. However, heirs from the royal lines are more skilled—that means they are gifted with one or more types of magic. On rare occasions, we will even have an elemental born witch; those are the ones that can manipulate the elements—earth, air, water, and fire." He paused and eyed me like he was waiting for me to ask questions. However, my brain was reeling with too much information, so I kept quiet.

"It's rare for a Caster to broadcast their talent. However, in my case, everyone knows that I have a knack for sensing another supernatural's natural energy. It's what landed me this job." He peered into my eyes and looked deep into me as if he was trying to read into my soul.

I shifted in my chair uncomfortably.

"I must admit that yours has me baffled. I've never felt one like it. Most especially, not in any Shifters," he continued.

"Can I come from two species?"

His head snapped up sharply, "No, interspecies breeding is not possible. Although there have been rare occasions that there were some interspecies relationships, they were never successful in producing children. It's believed that the genes are too incompatible to produce a child."

"Oh. So, I'm a weird Shifter then?" I said, feeling better. At least I knew what type of species I was and where I belonged.

He smiled. "I would definitely call you unusual. I will look into this more. I think we need to trace your parentage first if we want some answers. In the meantime, we need to study what your energy does, and this is the perfect setting for it. The king was right in sending you here."

I nodded, resigned to my fate. "You're right. I want to know where I came from."

"Excellent!" He beamed, then snapped his fingers and handed me a paper. "This is your schedule."

I took the paper and read my schedule. It looked like I had Shifter studies in the morning. Then on Mondays, Wednesdays, and Fridays, supernatural history and combat training before lunch and energy manipulation after lunch. On Tuesdays and Thursdays, I had independent studies all day.

I looked up, and the dean watched me closely with his hands clasped on top of the desk. "Do you have questions about your schedule?"

"Ah... yes, energy manipulation?" I asked with a frown.

"Yes, that will be with a one-on-one tutor. It will be with one of our advanced students. We need to uncover your dominant energy, and we need someone skilled in energy manipulation. We couldn't have you, a Shifter, mixed in with other Casters, so you will need to have private tutoring."

I nodded; his explanation made sense.

"For the other days, we allow our students the freedom to take on other subjects for independent studies, which they work on at their own pace. It is equivalent to college courses in the outside world. We have students pursuing jobs that require them to interact with humans routinely, so we need you to be as knowledgeable as the next human. You can enroll in any class you had planned to take at your local college back home. Some students continue their studies at a human college and finish their degree there once they have surpassed the limitations of what we could offer here."

I flashed him a big smile. I wasn't sure what I would major in, so I was glad I got to choose. "Are we limited to the number of independent classes we can take?"

"No. However, we have guides and recommendations based on your major. You can speak with counselors and tutors on the first level of the library. That's where you go if you need help and where you get checked off for your work. Here is a map of the campus. Read the book about our school history, rules, and regulations, so you know what to expect on your first day. You will also find your keys and any other pertinent information inside that binder. Everything you need should be in your room. Please know you are welcome to see me anytime," he told me, then got up and led me to the door.

"Thank you," I said before taking off and following the map to my room.

Chapter 4

Although my class wasn't until eight-thirty, I had been awake and dressed since seven in the morning. I packed my backpack with the tablet, a pen, and a binder and I grudgingly wore the uniform hanging in my closet. I had stayed up all night unpacking and gone to bed late, but my brain wouldn't shut down from worry. After less than five hours of sleep, I was wide awake at dawn. Restless energy coursed inside of me as I thought about what today would be like. *Maybe I should skip coffee this morning. I couldn't believe I had to go through the first day of school jitters again. I was an adult, for god's sake.*

However, the walk to my room last night had me dreading going to my classes. The school was as stuffy as I predicted. The students didn't look friendly; they had their noses turned up instead. Even the ones that didn't directly glare at me didn't even spare me a smile. It took me thirty minutes to find my damn room because no one bothered to help, and the place was enormous.

I clearly didn't belong in this school. Although I hadn't witnessed anything unusual, there was something different with the kids here compared to the ones in my high school. It was hard to describe in words, but I wouldn't necessarily think *supernatural.* I would just think these kids were weird. However, since I was aware that everyone was supernatural, I noted that they exuded power of some kind. Why didn't I ask

Rahl to tell me more about the supernatural world? I read the binder the dean gave and made sure I was aware of my schedule and the school rules. I also tried memorizing the map since I didn't want to draw any unnecessary attention to myself.

Done sitting in my room, anxiously waiting for the time, I left to eat breakfast in the cafeteria, which had been open since seven. Hopefully, there would be fewer people since no decent human being should be awake this early.

I brought my backpack just in case I got lost again, and the towers were across the quad, separated by the library and the gym. I needed to cross the large, open space with sloping grounds to get to the main building. From the map, there were different paths I could take. I didn't want to cross the open space, where students lingered and congregated, so I went through the trees leading to the back.

The cold sting of the morning air had me smiling and looking up at the tall willow trees where the birds chirped and sang their usual morning songs. I walked the pathway lined with greenery, and my head snapped to the side as I heard something scamper around the bushes. My steps halted as I waited for it to show itself. It sounded like a small animal. I strained my ears to listen, but despite how much Rahl insisted I just needed practice, my senses weren't as sharp as his. I should just ignore the animal as it probably wanted me to leave. However, I found myself inching slowly to where I heard the noise. When I rounded the bush, I saw a huge, white, long-eared bunny. *It was so stinking cute!*

"Aww... you scared me." I bent and picked up the cute chubby bunny and held it to my chest and I rubbed its head to calm it down. However, it frantically scrambled out of my arms, so I let it go. "I'm sorry. I didn't mean to frighten you."

As soon as I released it, the bunny shifted to a naked, petite girl with pin-straight black hair and brown eyes, glaring daggers at me.

My hand flew to my mouth. "Oh, my god. I am so sorry." I averted my eyes as my face burned from embarrassment.

She turned and grabbed her clothes from behind the bushes and started getting dressed. "Do you think this is funny, alpha?" She angrily yanked a shirt over her head and then put on her other clothes. "Is this one of your pranks? Make fun of the tiny bunny? Is that it?" Her voice got shrill, which had me looking back at her red face twisted in a scowl.

"Look. I am so, so sorry. I didn't mean to offend you. I didn't know you were a Shifter. I'm new." I stepped forward with my hands outstretched in a placating way.

"What kind of lame-ass excuse is that?" She crossed her arms and stood in front of me.

"It's the truth. I'm new, and I didn't know you were a Shifter. Otherwise, I wouldn't have done that. I'm so sorry. My name is Viola." I stretched out my hand.

She eyed it with a raised brow. "How can you not know I'm a Shifter?"

"I'm new to this school and to this world." I shrugged.

"That's not possible. You're an alpha."

"So, I've been told." I sighed and slowly lowered my outstretched hand.

She grasped it and said, "I guess I believe you since I don't smell any lie on you. I'm Shay Lee." She said it with a comical expression, like she didn't know if she should believe me and laugh or still be angry at me.

I beamed. *Finally, someone friendly.*

"Why are you here anyway, and why are you out this early?" Shay asked.

"I couldn't sleep, so I thought I'd check out the cafeteria."

"Good, I'm starving." She hooked her arm around me and led me to the cafeteria.

"So, when you say you're new to the supernatural world, what does that mean?" She eyed me sideways.

"I didn't know that supernaturals existed until a few months ago. I shifted for the first time then," I said casually as I picked a bowl of yogurt and fruit and placed it in my tray. I scooped some granola into it and then got a glass of orange juice and coffee.

I glanced at Shay, who was about five inches shorter than me. Her tray was laden with several plates of breakfast items. I raised my brows in question.

"What?" she asked in confusion.

"You're seriously eating all of that?"

She frowned. "Don't you eat a lot after your shift?"

"Oh, right. No. I don't seem to have that issue."

She opened her mouth to say something but just shook her head. We took a seat at the far corner, away from the food area and away from the entrance. The cafeteria was more like a fancy buffet rather than a school cafeteria. It was not like my school cafeteria, which had a peculiar smell to it. This place was bright and airy. The tables even had tablecloths on them. And the food didn't look like goo. Different varieties of food were laid out in stations and people went around picking up plates and cleaning up the tables.

Shay polished off her stack of pancakes in less than five minutes. She eyed my yogurt and pointed at it with her fork. "If my Shifter side couldn't sense your alpha wolf, I would say you were lying about being a Shifter. Even a normal Shifter couldn't sustain their energy with that few calories."

"What do you mean?"

"Even without shifting, our metabolism runs at a higher rate than a regular human. So, we have to consume more calories. Shifting itself is like running several marathons, so we need to stack up on calories after a shift, or we'll pass out."

"Interesting. No wonder Rahl always kept pushing me to eat." I spooned a blueberry in my mouth and shrugged.

Shay coughed and gagged on her food. She drank her juice and eyed me as she cleared her throat. "You mean, our king? King Fier? You're on a first-name basis with him?" She thumped her chest and coughed some more.

"Yes. I live there. He saved my life." I averted my gaze and grabbed the cup of coffee. I was about to lift it to my mouth to take a sip but paused. At the far end of the room sat two gorgeous guys who were staring at me. One had a snarl at his face, and the other had a look of curiosity.

I quickly averted my eyes as I felt my face burn.

Shay turned and followed my gaze to see what had my attention.

"I'm sure you know the princes if you live with the king?"

"Those are the heirs?" I whispered.

"How can you not know them if you live there?"

I sighed. "Look, I really don't like talking about it. My mom and I were on vacation from the country when we were attacked by a Vampire. Rahl saved me, but my mom didn't survive. That night was the first time I shifted. I had been with Rahl since. However, I've never met the princes."

She reached out and squeezed my hand. "I'm so sorry for your loss. This must be so frightening to you."

I nodded and blinked away the burning tears that threatened to fall.

She looked back one more time.

"Stop that."

She giggled, "Don't worry. They are used to the attention. As a matter of fact, they revel in it. However, they seem to not like you. They must not like having competition." She grinned.

"Please stop. I really don't want to call attention to myself." I looked at her tray to see if she was done. I wanted to get out of here. She had four empty plates stacked next to the two full plates of donuts, bacon, and eggs.

"I can't believe your tiny body can handle that much food." I stared in amazement.

"I can't believe you eat so little, and you're still walking around," she shot back.

"You make a cute bunny." I smirked.

She scrunched her nose and wiggled it just like a bunny.

I laughed and ignored the glares that were being thrown at me from the princes' table.

When Shay was finally done, we had just enough time to get to our class on time. "All Shifters meet at the hall. Then after the general announcements are made, we break into our rooms."

"How is that divided? Do you think we'll be in the same class?"

"No, alphas are in another class."

I halted and grabbed her arm. "You mean to say I'll be in a class with just the princes?"

"Lucky you! Every girl in school will want to trade places with you."

"Well, can we trade?" I asked seriously.

She tugged on my hand and said, "You'll be fine. Come on, or we'll be late."

"Did you not see the scowl on their faces? I'm sure they don't want me in their class."

"They don't have a choice. Just ignore them." She dragged me all the way to the hall as I tried to walk slowly, dreading being in the room with the scary princes.

As we entered the lecture hall, Shay marched down the stairs towards the front. I tugged her back and gestured for us to sit at the back. I was trying my best to ignore the stares from the other Shifters.

Shay rolled her eyes and grudgingly followed me as she muttered, "I like sitting in front so I can see."

"You'll be fine. I thought Shifters have enhanced senses," I said from behind my shoulder.

Thank goodness I chose the back, because a few minutes later, the two princes strolled in and sat directly in front of the professor. They walked in, acknowledging no one. The blond plopped on the chair while the brown-haired prince sat straight with an air of confidence no one could fake. I looked around and noticed the other girls staring at the two just like I was, so I forced myself to look to the front.

"Good morning, everyone. For those of you that don't know me, I'm Professor Wilkins, and I believe we need to welcome a new student. I'm sure everyone in this room has already recognized her alpha signature?"

Fuck. I sat lower in my seat and hunched over. Hopefully, the giant in front of me will hide me from the professor.

"Viola Price, please stand up and say hi to everyone."

I hunched even lower as I felt my face burn.

Shay tugged on my arm and pulled me to stand. The tiny five-foot-tall girl was freakishly strong. I stood and waved shyly, avoiding everyone's eyes.

"Ah, there you are. Welcome. It's a pleasure to have you in our class, Viola."

I smiled and sat before he finished his sentence.

"As you know, it's rare in our kind to have a female alpha, so the presence of one in this room is truly amazing. Please help me welcome Viola."

I sat in my chair and focused on getting my racing heart back to normal, so I hardly heard any of what the professor said. My pulse was just settling to a steady pace when Shay tugged at my hand. Everyone was out of their seats, making their way to their next class.

"Wait. I don't know where to go."

"Go talk to Professor Wilkins. I'll catch up with you at lunch." She waved.

I dodged bodies as they hurried out of the room while I trained my eyes on Mr. Wilkins, who was making his way to the door on his right. I sped up and caught him as he reached for the handle of the first door.

"Professor," I panted.

"Oh, hi, Viola. Come in." He held the door open for me.

I hesitated and looked up at him in question.

He chuckled. "I'm also your professor for the alpha Shifters' class."

"Oh, great. Thanks." I entered and halted as I was greeted with identical scowls from the princes. The brown-haired boy leaned on the wall by the window with his arms crossed and leg propped on the wall. The blond had his elbows resting on his legs and his fingers interlocked.

I stood rooted in the spot, avoiding their eyes.

"This is exciting," Professor Wilkins said as he shut the door, clearly unaware of the tension in the room. "We've never had a female alpha in the class, so this will make things interesting. Viola, you can have a seat anywhere. This is an informal class. The dean has informed me of your unusual circumstances, so I will give you a bit of a background about what we do in this class."

I nodded and peeked at the two handsome princes as I made my way to the far end of the room. They still had distasteful expressions.

"This class is to hone your individual shifting skills. We separate the class into different Shifters. From there, we group them into their level of shifting abilities. Since there are only a few alphas and your shifting abilities differ from the rest, we have a separate class for you. Plus, we are also doing this for the safety of the students."

I cocked my brow in question.

"When we shift, we give in to our basal animal instincts, and once we do, our animal wants to protect or to challenge. We can never predict when that happens and when a fight will ensue. Since an alpha never backs down and fights to the death, it's best to have you separated from the others."

Hopefully, these assholes can't hear my heart hammering from fear. I glanced sideways at them, and they flashed me sinister smiles. *Crap.*

"However, this class isn't only for shifting—which should be innate. It's also to learn control. We also enhance other shifting skills that could benefit you later. For example, we learn to make sure we don't lose our clothing when we shift from animal to human forms. Ultimately, the goal is to learn to be present or mentally aware while in our animal form. We want our beast and our human self to coexist."

My eyebrows drew together. I cleared my throat and looked around uneasily. "Can you please explain what you mean by that?"

"When we shift to our animal form, we give control to our wolf completely. They are in charge. It's like we are just passengers, but we are not in control. When you are truly one with your animal, you should be present during the shift. You will think and take an active role. That's when you are truly one with your wolf. There should be a seamless transition between forms without affecting your control."

I'd only shifted a handful of times, but that was how I already felt.

He must have seen the worry in my face because he asked, "What's wrong?"

I looked over at the two princes, who wore a bored expression, but they weren't fooling anyone. They sat too still to fake nonchalance.

"Don't be shy, Viola. This is a class where you need to be open. You are all allies here. There are only four of you in existence. The chances of producing an alpha heir from a traditional Shifter are very slim. For the alpha wolf line to continue, you three need to get along. The fate of the Shifters is in your hands," he said solemnly.

My jaw dropped. Did he just imply...? Now it was my turn to scowl.

Mr. Wilkins studied the three of us and bellowed a laugh. "Relax, you three. I didn't say you need to procreate now. Shifters live a long life. You can figure it out later."

Dear god, kill me now. I looked down at my intertwined fingers and studied them like they were the most exciting thing in the world.

"So, tell me what it is you wanted to say earlier."

I didn't look up from my fingers as I tried to formulate an answer.

"Come on, dear. How can I help you if I don't know what the problem is?"

"Well. It's just...the way you describe our, ah...animal. You know when you said we should feel awareness like we're one with our wolf?"

He nodded for me to go on.

"Well, I think...I mean...that's how I feel with mine."

He raised his brow in disbelief, so I hurriedly added, "I mean, I never really felt like there was a separate creature inside of me. I've heard it explained that there's supposed to be this thing inside of you, but I don't feel that." I shrugged.

I heard one prince snort.

The professor studied me closely. "That's interesting," Mr. Wilkins said. He tapped his jaw and asked, "Are you able to shift and keep your clothes?"

I had to think. "Yes. I mean, Ra...the king told me how to do it, but yes, the first time I shifted back, I had clothes on."

"That's impossible," one prince said. The one by the wall pushed off and faced me. He had blond, wavy hair, ocean blue eyes, and sinful red lips marred by his scowl. He rounded on me, and my hackles rose as he was radiating a lot of hostility. I recognized the posture. It was how Rahl had forced the shift in me—he was challenging me.

"Easy now, Sebastian."

"Oh, this will be fun," the other prince said.

I snarled but didn't break eye contact with the cocky prince that just challenged me. We both burst into our animal forms simultaneously, and Sebastian's wolf's eyes grew. Soon I heard a whimper escape his snout. I still felt threatened, so I showed my teeth and let a low growl escape. He broke eye contact and bounded for the door.

The other prince guffawed loudly, so I held his eyes captive and challenged him. I was done being bullied by these two. My challenge forced a quick shift from the second prince, who had the same reaction as Sebastian. The wolf took a step forward, but I let out a warning growl. If he stepped any closer, I would take a chunk off his leg. He halted and tucked his tail between his legs and eyed me. I kept growling. Until finally, he let out a whine and followed his brother out of the room.

It took me a moment to calm down.

When I no longer felt threatened, I noticed Mr. Wilkins, who was still in the room. I sniffed the air but didn't sense any aggression coming from him. With a cocked head, I studied Mr. Wilkins. His downcast eyes didn't meet mine. He then lifted his hands slowly and said, "I'm a friend, Viola."

I sat on my hind legs and continued to watch him.

His eyes grew in surprise. "Can...can you understand me?"

I nodded.

He couldn't hide his surprised expression. Well, I guess he didn't believe me earlier. I growled in response.

"I'm sorry. It's just unheard of. I've never witnessed anything like it. Actually, what happened with the princes earlier was shocking. The princes are known to never back down from a challenge. Can I ask you to shift back?"

I nodded once more and thought of my uniform as I shifted back to my body. Soon, I was standing in front of the professor.

His jaw hit the floor. "You weren't kidding," he whispered.

"Why would I kid about something like that?"

He was silent for a moment. "The dean told me about the dominant energy around you. I can't particularly sense it since your dominant alpha is overpowering and it makes my wolf uneasy. I'm certain it's what others feel around you, so don't be surprised if you get mixed reactions from your peers."

Well, that explained that.

"I'm still in shock. I've never seen two alphas back down from a challenge. I about peed my pants when you challenged each other. I thought I would have to call the dean over. As I said earlier, alphas fight to the death and those two are known to be brutal to their challengers. I can't believe they left and surrendered." He looked lost in thought. "You have a very dominant wolf in you, Viola."

"What happens now?"

"I will need to think about how to help you. You seem to instinctively know Shifter skills. However, the large hole in your past still holds you back from your true potential. We might need to focus on that. Maybe do some testing." We were both quiet for a moment. "Let me think about it and plan a different curriculum for you. For now, you are free to go. I'll see you back here next Wednesday."

"Thank you." I was glad to be out of the room. I don't even want to think about what happened with the princes. Thanks to the map, I found my way to supernatural history class. It was smaller than the hall, but it was larger than a regular classroom. I sat in the back, away from the occupied seats, and ignored the curious glances thrown my way. I kept my head down and doodled on my notebook as we waited for the professor.

I knew the room had slowly filled up with students by the level of noise, but I didn't dare look up. Finally, I heard the door shut, and my eyes grew in surprise when I saw a young professor.

He had dark hair cut short with the front perfectly coiffed in a curl, with dark brown eyes, and pink lips. Was he a vampire? He wore skinny black jeans rolled up over combat boots, a button-down shirt, and dark-rimmed glasses.

"Good morning, everyone." His eyes raked the class and settled briefly on me. "For those of you who don't know me, my name is Professor Taylor. I teach supernatural history. I take roll calls every morning, and if you are not here in time for that, don't bother coming in. I don't take late work and don't do make-up tests. I don't care what you do as long as you don't disrupt my class. It is up to you to pass or fail."

I straightened up and listened intently. As young as he looked, he didn't seem to be one to be trifled with. He took roll, and when he called my name, his eyes again lingered a second longer, which made me squirm in my seat.

"This year, we're going to cover the modern history of supernaturals."

A few people groaned in front.

He raised his eyebrows and asked, "What? You don't think it's important to learn about our recent history? Ms. Price, tell me why it's important to learn history?" His sharp eyes focused on me intently.

What the... My heart thundered, and my face burned. "Um... So, we can learn from our past?" I said hesitantly.

"Precisely. We study history not just to reminisce but to learn from our mistakes. Great historians believe that history always repeats itself. It's in our nature, whether humans or supernaturals. We have certain behaviors that have caused catastrophic events in history. Some call it our survival instincts. Others call it greed for power. Maybe it's both. That is what we will uncover this semester." His words were so profound that he commanded the room.

"Before we get into the nitty-gritty of modern history, let's do a recap. For those of you who already know this, feel free to tune me out." He smiled, which made him look cuter—like a nerdy, attractive professor.

"As far back as everyone remembers, the Casters always ruled the supernaturals. Perhaps because of their command of magic, they were believed to have the advantage—to be the most powerful amongst us. So naturally, they took power and commanded the supernaturals. The Vampires preyed on humans while the Shifters protected them against Vampires. Mostly, each race kept to themselves until the humans noticed the unusual deaths caused by Vampires. The Shifters implored the Casters to step in since they were supposed to be in charge. However, the Casters cared little for humans. They saw them as beneath supernaturals and not worth protecting. So, the Shifters revolted. War ensued between Shifters and Casters. The Vampires couldn't be bothered with the supernatural war. They just saw an opportunity. As the Casters and the Shifters warred, the Vampires pillaged whole towns. This was how humans discovered the existence of supernaturals." He looked around and paused. I followed his gaze and noticed everyone paying attention.

"The war between the Casters and Shifters got so bad that they brought on massive destruction to the humans. The humans then waged war on all supernaturals. They massacred us in great numbers. It took years of fighting. Each race's existence teetered at the brink of extinction before the three types of supernaturals banded together against the humans." There was silence in the room.

"They each chose a leader who was the strongest and most influential to represent them. This started the supernatural royalty. However, the royals' efforts were futile; the killing didn't stop. In a moment of desperation, the royals' only choice was to surrender to the human government.

"Hence the strict regulations and the segregation of supernaturals to this city—away from most humans." He paused once more to let it sink in. I looked around the room, and each of the students wore sad faces.

"So." His voice boomed, which made some of us jump in our seats. "This brings us to the current history of supernaturals. The creation of the royal lineage had untoward and unpredictable effects on all races. Now, the transfer of power only happens within their family line or through a duel to the death for the casters. Otherwise, the collective power of the race would wane or stay stagnant. With the Shifters, only the ones with alpha blood can lead them. If a non-alpha were to sit on the throne, the Shifters would stop producing younglings. The Vampires can only have a ruler within the same bloodline, all rulers can be traced back to the original king. If there is no ruling king from the bloodline, the entire race reverts to their blood-crazed bestial selves. In the past millennia, these scenarios have happened at least once. It was how it was discovered. We now need the royals for the survival of each race. We will visit those instances in detail."

The professor had everyone hanging on his words. Some listened intently, like me, while others took notes. I intended to take notes, but I didn't want to miss out on anything, so my paper stayed blank. I had never had a history class that didn't have anyone falling asleep. When the bell rang it was a surprise since I was so engrossed with the lecture.

"Ms. Price, a moment," Professor Taylor said.

I stopped and watched the last student file out of the room.

I anxiously shifted my bag from my shoulder as I faced the intimidating professor.

"Remember to learn from history." His brown eyes held mine as if they were conveying more than what he just said.

My brows furrowed, but I nodded in confusion. He went back to reading something on his desk, so I assumed I was dismissed. I frowned at him for a moment and then walked out.

What did that mean? Did he know my parents? I was walking back through the trees, with my thoughts consumed with what professor Tayler said, so I was startled to find the princes standing right in front of me, blocking my way.

I jerked to a stop and crossed my arms. "What do you want?"

"What did you do to us back there?" snarled Sebastian.

I cocked a brow. "What are you talking about?"

"My wolf...he's never acted that way before."

I snorted. "May I remind you that *you* challenged me?"

He eyed me slowly, in a sleazy way.

My hands balled into a fist.

"My uncle told me about you."

I splayed my hand on his chest to push him away, but my fingers grazed his exposed skin from an unbuttoned shirt and the sensation from our skin touching had both of us sucking in a startled breath. It felt like static electricity, but I felt it down to my bones.

Shaking off the weird sensation, I said in a low voice, "Don't force me to challenge you again."

Expecting his anger, I was surprised to see the longing in his piercing blue eyes. It was gone quickly. Then he stepped back and said, "Whatever." He dusted his shirt as if I had soiled him with my touch. "Let's go, Tris."

However, the other prince didn't move. He stood with his arms crossed, studying me with the same curiosity his wolf had.

"What?" I snapped.

"Who are you?" he whispered.

I froze, unable to answer. *Who was I?* Daughter of Mr. and Mrs. Price, or an adopted girl with unknown parents and an unknown past with mysterious powers. Our gazes locked, and I felt a particular connection to the blond prince. My heart rate spiked.

Still lost in each other's gaze, he stepped closer.

"Tris," Sebastian called, which broke the trance we were both in. He glanced at me one last time, then followed Sebastian.

I let out a loud exhalation and continued to make my way back to my room. *Weird.*

I plopped in bed, hoping that this day would go by with no more run-ins with either of the princes. With my eyes closed, I tried to forget about the disastrous morning, but my mind kept drifting back to Sebastian and Tristan—both too gorgeous for their own good. *Too bad they were assholes.* With a groan, I buried my face under a pillow. I couldn't possibly be attracted to those jerks, right? Nope, not happening.

I got up in annoyance and got ready for combat class. They allowed us to wear regular gym clothes, so I got my ass up and shrugged on a sports bra and leggings. I needed to get to class early to avoid those two.

Chapter 5

I found the class inside the gym building quickly enough. My steps echoed in the space while I walked into the reasonably large room that was about half the size of a basketball court. The walls were glass, and the bleachers were U-shaped. I sat on the right side, closer to the door, all the way on the top row. Leaning on the glass wall, I had a perfect view of the door while a post obscured me from sight to anyone entering. Students trickled in and barely paid me any attention. They scattered between the other two vacant bleachers. I wasn't sure if there was a seating arrangement, but no one had asked me to move.

I groaned internally when the two princes sauntered inside the room. Not looking in my direction, they situated themselves on the row in front of me, taking up almost half the bleachers.

Tristan leaned back on his elbow and glanced up at me with a broad smile on his face, which I ignored. Sebastian leaned forward on his knees and acted like I didn't exist, which was fine by me.

A couple of students squeezed themselves in at the end, away from the princes, while the other students who trickled into the room sat on the remaining open spots.

With still twenty minutes left before the class started, I leaned my head back on the wall and briefly closed my eyes. I tuned out the noise and ignored those who kept shooting glances at me as they whispered amongst each other.

A few minutes later, I heard a group of rowdy students enter, and a blanketed silence filled the room. My eyes snapped open, and my gaze landed on an emerald-green-eyed boy in front of the group. His gaze spoke of danger, passion, and mystery. He held my gaze, before my eyes assessed the rest of his features. He had dark hair and a pale face with pink lips and a chiseled jaw. I would have stared at him longer if the guys next to him didn't obnoxiously interrupt.

"What do we have here?" a large blond brute grinned with malice. He stopped in front of the princes, wearing a mischievous smirk and in a taunting voice asked, "Did the dogs adopt another alpha?"

I noticed the princes' shoulders tense up, but they otherwise ignored the jerk.

I rolled my eyes in response.

"Oh god. Not another one," a blond barbie said as she flipped her hair over her shoulder and crossed her arms.

"This is perfect. More mutts to practice on. Combat was getting boring," another guy with similar features to the first speaker said as he wiggled his eyebrows at me.

I ignored the group as my eyes darted back to the green-eyed boy. He glanced at the group and continued to walk to the opposite bleachers. The rest of the group followed while the two guys and the girl stayed.

"Get back to your seat, Logan, before I make you," Tristan hissed in a low voice.

"Ohh. I'm terrified," Logan said with a puffed-up chest.

Tristan stood and towered over him with narrowed eyes and a clenched jaw.

Logan's eyes turned red which made me freeze, as it took me back to the night my mother was attacked. I would never forget those red eyes that stared at me as he clutched my bleeding mother to his chest. Pure rage filled me. "Vampire," I hissed before I launched myself at Logan. I felt myself partially shift, and my fingers turned into sharp claws as my hands wrapped around Logan's neck. I landed on top of him while we slid into the middle of the room. My wolf's vision narrowed on the Vampire's face, and my sharp teeth protruded from my mouth. The need to rip out his throat took over. But I didn't want to see a repeat of what was done to my mother. Plus, killing him quickly was merciful. This Vampire needed to suffer as my mother had suffered. He struggled to breathe. Both his hands grabbed onto mine as he tried to rip my hands off his neck. But I had a vice grip hold on him, and I wouldn't budge no matter how much he bucked. I gladly looked at the blood dripping down his neck. This time it wasn't my mother's blood. It was the Vampire's as my claws dug deeper into his neck.

A female shrieked close to my ear before her hand landed hard on my shoulder. I released one hand while the other kept a firm grip on his neck, then I reached back at the hand on my shoulder and yanked it away from me. I heard bones breaking, followed by her scream. I spared her a glance and bared my teeth at the blonde barbie while a warning growl began deep in my chest. Her cries turned to a wail as she scrambled away from me. She remained where she was sitting, cradling her injured hand before I allowed myself to look away.

My attention snapped forward as I felt an attack but didn't bother looking. Instead, I thrust my hand forward on instinct and heard a crash.

My attention focused on my prey, whose blood pooled underneath him as his neck continued to bleed while his face turned blue. His hold on my hand was getting weaker.

"Viola, stop. Please," someone said.

"Viola, come back to us. Don't do this," said another.

I cocked my head and looked around, searching for the voices, and saw the princes holding back the other boy who had taunted me. He struggled to get to me. My hackles rose as his red eyes met mine, his face twisted into the same vicious anger as the monster that took my mother from me.

"Vampire," I snarled, casting a look at the boy below me. I was about to lunge at the other Vampire when another voice burst through my angry mist.

"Jacob. Stop. Stand down. You're making it worse," the voice commanded.

I searched for the speaker, and it was emerald-eyes. His pleading eyes looked back at me. Next to him was a tall, lanky boy with ruffled hair. I looked around the other students as they huddled in a corner with an old man in front of them.

"Viola, please release him," Tristan asked.

"You don't want to do this," Sebastian begged, frowning, which twisted his beautiful face.

I looked back at Logan, who ceased to struggle. He gasped for air, and his hands were limp at his sides. I eased up on the hold on his neck and slowly got up. Barbie flinched as I glanced her way, then my eyes landed on Jacob. "I hate Vampires. If you are one, stay away from me."

I heard the emerald-eyed boy suck in a sharp breath, which I ignored as I made my way out of the room.

My anger was still under my skin as I crossed the quad.

"Viola, wait up."

I turned and saw Tristan jogging up to me.

I kept walking, but he caught up with me.

"What do you want?" I snapped.

"Are you okay?"

I paused, taken aback by his kind tone and the concerned look on his face. It took me a minute to answer. The adrenaline was slowly leaving my system, and anger was now mixed in with worry.

"Did I kill him?"

"No. Vampires heal fast." His lips quirked. "But you came close to it."

"Am I going to be in trouble?" Shame seeped into me as the reality of what I'd done hit me.

"I don't know," he said, the smile vanishing from his face.

We padded to my dorm, vulnerability still filled me and didn't want to be alone at the moment, so I asked, "Do you want to come in?"

He flashed me a grateful smile and nodded. He looked around the room and said, "Huh, I guess they give all the alphas the same room."

"What do you mean?" I looked around the dorm room where a couch sat by the entrance and to the right was a breakfast area next to the window with a small kitchenette, then the door to the bathroom which connects to the bedroom with a decent size walk-in closet. "Doesn't everyone have the same room?"

He shook his head. "No, some have a single, and others have a double and a shared bathroom. Only a few have a suite."

"Oh," I said, shocked that the academy gave me a nice room. I needed to thank Rahl for all of this. A pang of guilt hit me at my behavior. It was a low way of repaying him. "Will this cause problems for Rahl?" I asked as I sat heavily on the couch.

Tristan sat next to me and nudged my knees with his. "Hey, don't worry. It won't be as bad as you think. That wasn't the first time there's been a fight in school. Especially in combat class."

I looked up at him skeptically. "Are you sure?"

"Yes. We're Shifters. Vampires are our natural enemies. Logan got cocky. He shouldn't have challenged an unknown alpha."

"You mean, shit like that happens all the time?" My brow rose in question.

His lips quirked up cutely. "I mean, not to that degree, but yes. Pretty much." He shrugged.

"I don't think I want to be a part of that. I meant what I said," I whispered and crossed my arms.

He studied me for a moment but didn't ask, which I appreciated. "Do you want to go to the cafeteria and eat something? Everyone is still in class, so it will be empty."

I considered his offer and nodded.

He flashed me a smile, and my stomach fluttered. This guy was too gorgeous and should come with a warning.

"Are you okay?"

I felt his eyes on me, but I looked ahead and simply nodded.

"Do you want to talk about it?"

I shook my head.

"That's cool," he said.

I peeked at him, and he kept his hands inside his pockets.

We walked in silence for a few minutes.

"That was some badass partial shift, though." He smirked and held the door open for me.

My lips quirked at his teasing.

"Seriously, Seb and I just learned to partially shift a few years ago. And we still have trouble sometimes when we're emotional."

My eyebrows rose.

He handed me a tray, and I picked up a salad and a sandwich. He paused and eyed my tray but said nothing. He loaded his with several plates, and after we filled our glasses with drinks, we took our seats.

"So, are you really new to all of this?"

I cocked an eyebrow.

He grinned, which made my heart flutter. "Hey, I had to ask."

He polished off several plates before I was even finished with my salad.

I chewed on my sandwich quietly. My stomach was in knots as I worried about the consequences of my actions.

I felt Tristan's warm hand on mine, and his gunmetal blue eyes held me captive. "Stop. It's gonna be okay. I promise." He squeezed my hand and released it.

My fingers twitched, missing his warmth. I smiled and continued to pick at my sandwich. After eating half of it, I pushed it away and noticed Tristan's cocked eyebrow.

I rolled my eyes. These Shifters really had issues with food.

He grabbed his cup of pudding and took a couple of bites, then offered me a spoonful. My eyes grew in surprise. He was practically a stranger, and he was offering to spoon feed me dessert. I hesitantly opened my mouth and took a bite.

"Wow, that's delicious."

His smile grew, and he insisted on feeding me the whole cup.

"What is it about you Shifters and food?"

"I don't want you to pass out. You expelled a lot of energy back there, so you need the calories."

"I'm fine. I'm not very hungry."

He shook his head. "There's no such thing," he said as he continued to polish off the rest of his plate. "Okay, we should take off if you want to avoid the crowds."

"You don't have to stay with me, you know."

"Nonsense. There's no place I'd rather be."

"But, where's your twin?"

"Twin?" He frowned.

"The other prince. You two are so similar, and every time I see you, you're always together." I shrugged.

He laughed. "Wait till Seb hears about this."

"Where are we going?"

"Well, we have an hour to kill, so we can either hide out in the library, but there's a chance that we'll run into someone, or we can go back to your room or mine."

I raised my brow skeptically.

He chuckled. "I wish, but now is not the time." Then he draped an arm on my shoulder and leaned close to my ear. "Maybe next time."

I elbowed his rib, and he laughed and released me.

He grabbed my hand and said, "Come on."

I trailed behind him as my face burned from his flirting.

His dorm was two floors above mine and, as he'd said, looked similar. "Huh. I thought you lived with your brother."

"His room is next door," he said as he picked up the room. There were books, dirty dishes, magazines, and clothes scattered around the room.

He pointed to the couch and carried a load of mess in his arms to his bedroom.

"What's your next class?"

"Energy manipulation."

He frowned. "Are you sure? Shifters don't normally take that class."

"Yeah." I sighed and leaned my head back on the couch. "Add another thing weird about me."

The couch dipped next to me, and he grabbed my hand and played with it. My chest tightened, and I peeked at him from under my lashes. "What are you doing?"

"I don't think you're weird. I think you're fascinating," he whispered and continued to play with my fingers.

My heart stuttered as I watched him. He kept his head bowed and focused on our hands. His hair fell into his eyes, and I longed to brush it off to the side.

He peeked at me from under his naturally long, thick lashes, which cast shadows on his cheek, and my pulse started racing. The air got heavy, and his gaze darted to my lips. We naturally leaned towards each other, our breaths mixing, which was intoxicating. My eyes fluttered close as our lips touched in a featherlight kiss. That brief contact caused all of my senses to go on hyper-drive. I wanted more of him. I opened my mouth to deepen the kiss, but then the door banged opened, and we both jumped apart. We were breathing heavily as we looked at each other.

"What is going on?"

We turned to a scowling Sebastian. For a moment, I thought I saw jealousy, but I must have been mistaken.

"Sup, man?"

"I've been searching all over for the two of you."

"Why?" I asked.

"The dean wants a word."

Fear replaced the desire flooding my veins.

"What's going on? Did he say why?" Tristan asked.

"No. Just that she needed to go there quickly." Sebastian shrugged.

Tristan grabbed my hand and said, "Don't worry, Vi. I'll go with you."

I forced a smile, but words failed me. I stared at the two princes with panicked eyes.

Sebastian narrowed his eyes towards our connected hands and looked away, jaw tight and shoulders stiff.

Tristan tugged on my hand. "Let's go. Might as well get it over with."

I allowed Tristan to drag me to the door as my mind raced over the possibilities of my punishment.

"If you're going, then I'm going," Sebastian said with a slight jut of his jaw.

I didn't care what he did. I might get kicked out of the academy, or worse, I might go to jail.

I clutched Tristan's arm as he knocked on the dean's door. Apparently, the princes had certain privileges since the secretary didn't bat an eye when we walked past her.

The door swung open, but no one was behind it. The dean sat in his chair, and two boys occupied the seats in front of his desk. The princes didn't seem surprised by the door, so I ignored it. My mind quickly moved on to the people in the room. The boy with emerald eyes from the gym sat in front of the dean, and on the other seat sat the tall guy with unruly hair. The princes stiffened up at the sight of the other two.

"Dean, you called?"

He sighed heavily. "I called for Viola. Not all of you." He massaged the bridge of his nose and leaned back in his chair. He rested his intertwined fingers on top of his stomach, and after a long pause, he said, "What are we going to do about this?"

"About what, exactly?" Tristan asked. He stood with his hands crossed and his legs spread apart. We stood behind the two boys with Tristan on my right and Sebastian on my left.

"Why are they here?" Sebastian snarled.

The boy with emerald eyes narrowed his gaze at the princes while the other, older boy ignored them.

"Viola, have you met Kol and Carlisle?"

I shook my head.

"Viola, this is Kol Dandridge, prince of the Vampires, and Carlisle Parker, heir to the former head of the coven. Everyone knows who Viola is."

I appraised Kol, who looked tense as he gripped the chair arms tightly. I waited for the anger to fill me as it did earlier, but all I had was curiosity towards the prince. I nodded in acknowledgment and saw him visibly relax. I turned towards Carlisle; whose warm, hazel eyes crinkled on the side as he flashed me a smile.

"Am I in trouble?" I asked the dean.

"That's why we are all here, Viola. We want to stop this from getting out. We don't want the royals getting involved."

"Again, why are they here?" Sebastian copied Tristan's posture and glowered at everyone in the room.

"We're here to help Viola," Kol said.

"I doubt that," Tristan said.

And Sebastian followed with, "Why is witch boy involved?"

Carlisle chuckled. "You don't know, do you?"

"What do you mean?" I asked, looking between the three in front of me.

The dean let out a loud breath and stood. "Let's all get comfortable and sit while we discuss it further." He walked around his desk and sat in one of the comfortable couches in front of the fireplace, gesturing for us to follow.

After a moment of hesitation, Tristan took the long couch, and I opted for the single seat, but Sebastian steered me next to Tristan, then sat next to me. I raised an eyebrow in question, but he ignored me.

The other two took the love seat across from us.

"I wanted to speak with Viola alone, but I appreciate all of you wanting to help. As you know, we are in a precarious situation. If the royals get involved, this might turn into a political issue."

"Why would it? It's not uncommon for a fight to break out in school," Tristan said as he waved his hand. He looked relaxed with his legs crossed, and his arm casually rested on the back of the couch, while Sebastian still had his arms crossed as he sat stiffly on the sofa.

Kol snorted. "It's not every day that a prominent family in the Vampire clan almost gets murdered."

"It's also not common that an alpha takes on several Vampires and a wizard," Carlisle said as he leaned forward with raised brows.

My forehead scrunched. "What are you talking about?" I looked at Kol, the dean, and then the princes. "I didn't..." *What is he talking about?*

"I've been meaning to ask you, Viola. How did you do it?" Carlisle asked.

"Do what? I did nothing," I snapped.

"I tried to get you off, Logan, but you deflected my power and threw it back at me." He cocked his head and studied me.

I opened my mouth to disagree, then I remembered the feeling of being attacked and remembered the energy I pushed and the crash I heard. I snapped my mouth shut and leaned back.

Carlisle smiled triumphantly.

Tristan straightened up. "What does it mean?"

"That's what we're here to figure out, Mr. Cormel. King Rahl and I have been aware of the unknown dominant energy radiating from Viola. We hoped that the knowledge of her parentage would answer that mystery, but after today, it just got more complicated."

"What dominant energy?" Sebastian asked.

"Aside from the alpha energy, there is a more dominant energy inside of her," the dean answered. He turned to Carlisle. "Can you feel it?"

"Yes. But it's unfamiliar; I've never felt that kind of power," Carlisle said, still eyeing me curiously.

The dean nodded. "Will your parents be a problem?" He directed the question to Kol.

He shrugged. "If they find out then, yes."

Sebastian snorted next to me.

"Can you control your crew to keep it within the school grounds?" Mr. Wilson urged.

He thought for a minute. "The boys, yes, but Carla? I'm not so sure."

"Isn't she your fiancé?" Tristan snarled.

Kol glanced at me with regret in his eyes.

I wasn't sure why, but my heart contracted in pain at the word fiancé. This was my mortal enemy. Who cared if he was destined to marry the wench?

"Yes, shouldn't that count as something? Make her stay quiet," Carlisle said to everyone's surprise. He seemed like a serious, rule-abiding person.

"What about you? Can you control your coven to stay quiet? That was some impressive show of power," Kol snapped.

"Wait. Why are you two protecting Viola?" Sebastian asked.

"Not that we're ungrateful, but it's suspicious, you see," Tristan followed. Did they always finish each other's sentences like that? I looked from one to the other. However, they had a point.

"You can trust them," the dean said in a tone that conveyed that there would be no more discussion regarding the matter.

"Now, what will we do about Viola's issue?" Kol asked.

"Excuse me?" I twisted and raised a brow at Kol.

"Well, your hatred of Vampires started this total mess. Who's saying that this won't happen again?" He looked at me coldly.

I straightened up and reminded myself that he was the enemy. "You're still standing, aren't you?"

Tristan chuckled while Sebastian groaned.

Carlisle was trying hard to suppress his smile.

The dean, however, looked grave. "He has a point, Viola. Will there be a repeat of this incident?"

My anger dissipated as fast as it came, replaced by uncertainty and guilt. "I don't know," I said in a small voice.

"Can you tell us what happened?" the dean asked.

I shrugged. "I don't like Vampires."

Kol flinched then clenched his jaw.

"That's not entirely accurate," Carlisle said.

"How the hell do you know, witch boy?" Tristan said.

"Bear with me, Viola. But I have a theory. I was studying the whole interaction, but I kept my eye on you throughout." My stomach fluttered with his words. I couldn't meet his eyes, so I peeked at him from under my lashes. "You didn't react until you noticed their eyes change. As a matter of fact, you only reacted to Logan because he was the only one who was being aggressive. The others, while Vampires, didn't trigger your response. It was the aggressive Vampire that made you act."

I thought back, and he was right. "Yes, I believe you're right. Those red eyes triggered something in me."

"We should test this theory," Tristan said with a wide grin.

Everyone turned their heads in his direction and stared at him like he had gone crazy.

"What? We need to be sure." He shrugged.

"I don't think I can risk the prince in an experiment," Mr. Wilson said.

"Oh, I'm sorry, sir. Is the Kol too precious?" Tristan asked with mock innocence.

Kol clenched his fists and said with gritted teeth, "We can test it. I'm not scared." His breathing came in short bursts, and then his eyes flashed red. Then he directed his angry gaze at me.

Once again, I froze, and memories of that horrible night surfaced. Instinctually, my fingernails lengthened into sharp claws, which pierced my skin as I had my hands balled in anger. The pain had me taking deep breaths to keep a clear mind, so I could control myself and not attack Kol. I growled but stayed seated. The pain in the palm of my hands kept me present. I felt an energy threat directed at me once again, and on instinct, I thrust my hand out and blocked it. I felt another attack come from my left and did the same. This time I heard a grunt, and a body hit the wall along with the furniture.

"Holy shit!"

"Viola!"

Kol's eyes returned to their gorgeous emerald green, and after a moment, I felt my fangs and claws retreat. I looked around to see that something wrapped Carlisle with an energy field while the dean laid against the wall at an awkward angle with half of the room blown to pieces.

My hand slapped my mouth. "Oh my god. Please tell me he's okay."

"Viola, release me so I can help him." Carlisle banged on the energy dome.

I looked at him helplessly, then looked at Kol and the princes for help. They shrugged.

"I don't know how," I cried.

"Call the energy back to you."

"What?"

"Just do it," he snapped.

I concentrated and felt for the energy like I did before, but I pulled instead of pushed. It took me at least three times before he could break it on his own. He then rushed to the dean and ran his hands up and down his body. "Kol, I need your help."

I hovered behind Carlisle as my body shook. Tristan pulled me against his chest, and I clutched at it in fear for the dean. "It's gonna be okay," he whispered and kissed the top of my head.

Kol pierced his finger and let his blood drip inside the dean's mouth.

Slowly, color returned to the dean's cheeks, and then his eyes fluttered. He sat up and blinked slowly. I threw myself on the floor and sobbed. "I'm so sorry. I didn't mean to..." I hiccupped.

He patted my shoulder and said, "It's alright. I should have known better than to throw energy at an unknown threat. I'm old enough. That was a rookie mistake."

Kol pulled Mr. Wilson to his feet, while Tristan did the same to me. The dean waved his hand, and the room returned to its pristine state. We took our usual seats, and I kept my head bowed.

"What just happened?" Sebastian asked.

"Why didn't the witch boy get thrown into the wall like the dean?" Tristan followed with a glint in his eye.

I watched Carlisle's reaction, but he just ignored Tristan.

"I would like to know the same thing." The dean's brow furrowed. "Viola, can you walk us through what happened?"

I nodded. If it meant preventing innocent people from getting harmed, then yes. I would divulge anything they wanted. "I was concentrating on not attacking Kol. However, I felt a threat and reacted. I didn't think. I just reacted. In the classroom, I wasn't even aware I used magic." I looked up from twisting my fingers. "That's what I did, right? I used magic?"

The two Casters nodded, their frowns and discomfort evident.

"That's impossible," Kol said in a low voice.

"Wait, are you two implying that she's a hybrid?" Sebastian asked.

"No, we don't know that," the dean said with a sigh.

"We only know that she can shift and that she can wield magic," Carlisle said.

"So, we still don't know what I am?"

"No, but it's even more imperative to find your parentage. If the royals and the coven leader find out what you can do, they will be very interested in you. Please try not to draw any attention in the meantime. I'm your assigned tutor for energy manipulation, so we'll work on your control." Carlisle said.

"I suggest you work with Kol on controlling your anger towards Vampires," the dean advised.

Kol's jaw clenched, and he gave a curt nod.

"We'll be there to help," Sebastian said with narrowed eyes.

"It still doesn't answer why witch boy was safe inside his energy cocoon while the dean lost consciousness," Tristan asked.

"Actually, the same thing happened in the classroom. The other casters were all sprawled out in the room while witch boy was safe inside of the cocoon," Sebastian said.

"I have a theory," Carlisle said.

"Another one?" Kol asked, heavy with sarcasm.

The twins shared a smirk but said nothing.

"I don't think Viola feels threatened by the four of us. We were the only ones who could come close to her during her...episode. Everyone else was fair game. I mean, it's just a theory which still needs to be tested, but..."

"Is that true?" The dean directed the question at me.

I thought about it. "I don't know. I didn't really think. I just reacted and with Kol, I tried hard not to attack him. I didn't try with Logan."

"We will need to test that theory somehow," Kol said with a frown. "I'll think of something.

After a few minutes of silence, the dean said, "Okay, it doesn't need to be said, but let's keep this between us." He got up and led us to the door.

Tristan waited outside, followed by Kol, who walked out without a backward glance. "Bloodsucker," Tristan snarled as he passed by. Then he turned to Carlisle and said, "Witch boy." Carlisle also ignored him.

We joined Tristan, and we walked back to the dorm quietly.

"Do you think it's safe to leave Viola alone?" Tristan asked.

Sebastian snorted. "I think we should worry about others' safety."

"Hey."

Tristan snickered. "He's right, you know."

"Whatever."

We got to my dorm, and the princes didn't look like they were ready to leave. I hesitated and then invited them in.

"Is there something you need?" I asked as I stood behind the single-seat while the two lounged on the long couch.

"Yes. Will you tell us what your issue is with Vampires?" Sebastian asked.

I crossed my arms around my body and chewed on my lip. My chest felt heavy from the memory of that night as if it knew that I was about to recall the worst pain I'd ever experienced. Finally, I sat heavily on the couch and, after a moment, said, "I met Rahl the night I lost my mother. He saved me from a Vampire," I whispered. "That was the first time I found out I was a Shifter and that supernaturals were real. I lost everything that night because of a Vampire," I said with clenched fists and fire in my chest.

Tristan squeezed his giant ass next to me and held me tightly. "I'm so sorry, Vi."

His embrace felt nice and comforting. I let out a loud breath along with the tension I carried inside of me, then saw Sebastian watching us. He had a look in his eyes that I couldn't recognize, but for once, it wasn't hostile.

We sat in silence for a few minutes, then Sebastian stood and stretched.

"Are you gonna be okay?" Tristan asked.

I nodded.

"We'll see you tomorrow, Vi," Sebastian said.

My stomach fluttered with Sebastian calling me Vi. I smiled and walked them out.

I leaned on the door and, for once, felt excited and looked forward to a new day in the academy. I looked forward to spending more time with Tristan. I didn't know what was brewing between us, but he stuck with me all day, and he made me feel special. It was also nice to not be hated by Sebastian.

Chapter 6

I came early and sat nervously on the bench where I first met Shay, hoping to catch her before breakfast. My legs bounced as I kept glancing in both directions. I worried she wouldn't want to be my friend after hearing about what happened yesterday.

My head snapped toward heavy footsteps, and I saw Shay walking with a girl about my height with an athletic body, brown skin, and brown hair. Here goes nothing. Wiping my sweaty palms on my jeans, I stood up and met them halfway. My anxiety eased as Shay flashed me a big smile.

"Hey, Viola. I'm glad you're here. Where were you yesterday? This is Lori. Lori, Viola."

"Hi." I smiled at Lori.

"Hi," she said as she averted her eyes. Great, she probably heard about what happened yesterday and was afraid of me.

"We're headed to breakfast. Wanna join us?" Shay asked.

"Are you sure? I don't want to intrude." I glanced at Lori, but her expression remained blank.

"Oh. Relax." Shay waved her hand in the air. "I told you she's nice."

Lori's face flushed, and she glared at Shay. Yep. She'd definitely heard about the incident. My heart sank. "You heard about yesterday?"

"Girl, the entire school heard about yesterday. I don't think anyone will dare mess with you after that show." Shay chuckled as she hooked her arm around mine.

"Logan was a bully, and he challenged my wolf." I shrugged.

"Yeah, that bloodsucker deserved it," Lori said. My head snapped in her direction with my brows raised.

"You have issues with vamps as well?" My tone was surprised as I studied her relaxed shoulders and the faint smile on her lips. Perhaps she was just shy earlier.

"Just the bullies." She shrugged.

"Yeah." I breathed as my shoulders relaxed. I smiled at Shay, glad to have her by my side.

Shay and Lori piled their trays with several plates while I picked my usual yogurt with fruit and granola.

Lori raised an eyebrow, and I cut her off. "Don't start. I already get enough shit from everyone about my diet." I scooped a bite of strawberry in my mouth.

She shrugged and said nothing. I might actually like this girl.

"So, how did you two meet?" Lori asked.

"Oh my god—"

"Don't do it!" Shay glared at me as my mouth opened to answer.

"What?" Lori asked and looked between the two of us.

My lips turned up, and Shay shook her head and slouched over her plate. "I picked up what I thought was a cute, fluffy bunny and petted it. The next thing I knew, it turned into a feisty girl," I said, failing to keep the laugh that bubbled up from my mouth.

Lori burst out laughing while Shay glared at the two of us, but she failed to hide the smile on her face.

"Oh my god." Lori laughed as she clutched her stomach. She tried speaking a few times but couldn't say a word from laughing so hard. Finally, she wiped tears from her eyes and sniggered. "I would have loved to have seen that."

"No, you wouldn't," Shay huffed. "Well, let's hope she doesn't pet you next."

"What do you shift into?"

"A black panther," Lori said proudly as she finished her cup of oatmeal.

"Wow. That's impressive. And no, I wouldn't want to pet a panther."

Lori looked at me like I was crazy.

"What?"

"You really are new to all of this, huh?"

"She can pet me anytime." Tristan pulled up a chair and squeezed in between Lori and me. He then turned to me and wiggled his brows.

I giggled and rolled my eyes. "In your dreams."

Sebastian stood behind him wearing his usual scowl. "We're heading to class. We wanted to make sure you sat with us," he said when I turned in his direction.

I stared at him with a raised eyebrow. "I'm not sitting in front. Plus, I wanna stay with these two. I'll meet up with you guys after." I pointed to Shay and Lori, who sat awkwardly, avoiding the princes' eyes.

"Fine. Let's go, Tris."

"Aww. C'mon. Vi," Tristan said, ignoring Sebastian.

"Nope. I don't like sitting in front. Go," I said, shaking my head as I pushed on his firm shoulder. He eventually stood up with a pout. I chuckled as I watched them go.

I paused when I noticed Shay and Lori gape at me with wide eyes. "What?"

"We've never seen the princes friendly with anyone." Shay said as she gaped at me.

"Yeah, it was weird. They're normally so broody. And they stick to themselves." Lori stacked her empty plates and dabbed her mouth with a napkin.

"I know what you mean. They were mean to me at first, but I think they're warming up." I was glad to hear they weren't just assholes to me. Although, I still wasn't sure about Sebastian. He had changed a little.

As we got up, I paused at the suddenly quiet cafeteria. It was like someone pressed the mute button. Students peered at me surreptitiously. Then the silence broke, and a cacophony of whispers filled the room. Shay grabbed my arm as we walked at a brisk pace out the door. I kept my head high and ignored them, but I caught a few glares from those I suspected were Vampires. However, no one dared to say anything.

Shay and Lori flanked me on each side and kept throwing glances at me, but I just marched ahead in silence. I wasn't too bothered by everyone else in school; I was okay as long as I had a few friends.

As we entered the room, Shay made her way down the stairs, but I tugged on her elbow and pointed to the seats towards the back. She rolled her eyes but made her way to our previous seats. She paused before taking a seat. I wondered what was going on, so I looked over her shoulder and saw Tristan and Sebastian sitting one row in front of us.

"Hey, guys. Why are you back here?" I called and nudged Shay's back to keep going.

Sebastian crossed his arms and scooted lower down his seat, "Isn't it obvious? We're here because he wants to sit next to you." He jerked his thumb towards Tristan.

I looked towards Tristan for confirmation. He nodded his head, wearing a broad grin on his face.

I flashed him a big smile as I took my seat.

The students entering paused and glanced at the princes and then back at me before they took their seats.

"Great. Because of your stunt, you're calling unnecessary attention to me," I leaned forward and hissed between the princes.

"Exactly," Sebastian said in a gloating voice.

"Oh, shut up. No one made you sit here. Why are you two joined at the hip, anyway?" I snapped, annoyed with the constant attention I was getting.

The girls snickered next to me but cut it short as Tristan side-eyed them.

I looked up at the professor, who had been talking for the past twenty minutes. He had his eyes trained in our direction. He met my eyes and flashed me a disapproving look, so I straightened up and tried to concentrate on what he was saying. However, I was too upset to absorb any information. *Why couldn't I just blend in? I didn't need this extra attention.* I spent the rest of the class so consumed with annoyance that I jumped when everyone stood and made their way to their individual classes.

"We'll see you at lunch," Shay said as she and Lori made their way to their class.

"Sorry about calling attention to you," Tristan whispered in my ear. He was close enough to feel his lips on my skin, which peppered my skin with goosebumps.

This boy was smooth. He knew how to make a girl feel better. My mood had lightened up, so I said, "It's not your fault. Everyone has been looking at me weird and whispering everywhere I go. It's just getting old." I sighed and wished I was back with Rahl searching for my past instead of being subjected to this shit.

Tristan grasped my hand as he led me to Professor Wilkin's room. I peeked at him from under my lashes, but he looked straight ahead with a slight smile on his lips.

When we entered the room, Sebastian's eyes narrowed and zeroed in on our clasped hands. His scowl deepened, and he pretended to ignore us as we got closer and sat behind him.

"How's everyone today?" Professor Wilkins asked after he set his stuff down on the table. His brows rose in question when no one answered. "Alrighty, then. Since you three are about at the same level of power, we'll just pick up where we left off."

Great. Why did he have to call attention to my powers? I glanced at Sebastian, and as expected, he didn't look happy with the statement. My heart sunk. I thought we made progress yesterday. Apparently, we were back to hating each other again.

My elbow rested on the table, and my chin sat on my palm as I concentrated on Professor Wilkins' explanation of the alpha's command. My neck prickled as Tristan twisted the ends of my hair. I squirmed at the sensation traveling down my spine and hid a smile that was threatening to escape. I really enjoyed his affection. I didn't think I would like a very touchy guy, but with Tristan, it was terrific. Not that I had much experience with dating since I had been busy working, but I'd had some boyfriends when Dad was alive. Although, I wouldn't call them a proper relationship like I heard the girls at school gossip about. I just remembered thinking how much trouble it was to be in a relationship since the girls gushed over their boyfriends one minute and then cried over stupid things. Mine was innocent. We hung out and maybe shared a kiss. Then again, I was very young.

I peered at Tristan, who absently kept his hand on my hair as he listened to Mr. Wilkins. My stomach fluttered, and I averted my gaze back to the front. Tristan elicited strong feelings inside of me, which brought a sudden flood of fear. Getting attached to Tristan would complicate things with Sebastian. I needed all the allies I could get and to not make any more enemies. It was hard enough with everyone hating me.

Tristan leaned forward, his warm breath tickling my ear, which had me sucking in a breath. "What's wrong?"

"You two, stop flirting, and please pay attention," Professor Wilkins said with a twinkle in his eyes.

Sebastian looked absolutely livid. If he was capable, smoke would be pouring out of his ears. The tips of his ears were red, and his fists were clenched. What was his problem? Was he worried that I was stealing his brother's attention?

The rest of the class went by with no other incident. Professor Wilkins went on about the history of the alpha's command, the science behind it, and some examples in battles.

It was the same boring stuff I glazed over when Rahl tried to teach me about Shifters' history.

I spent the rest of the class enjoying Tristan's touches and studying Sebastian's tense profile. I couldn't figure out why he was friendly yesterday, and today he was back to hating me.

When Professor Wilkins dismissed us, I was out of my seat and darted to the door. I didn't want to deal with Sebastian.

"Hey, Vi. Wait up."

"I'll catch up with you later, Tristan. I don't want to be late." I called back to him. I darted out of the room and took the stairs two at a time. As I reached the top of the stairs, someone grabbed my elbows.

"Hey, what's going on?" Tristan asked with a frown. "Did I make you feel uncomfortable back there?"

"I...No." I looked around the empty classroom hall and finally met his piercing blue eyes.

"Why are you avoiding me, Vi?" He fixed his eyes on me.

My heart galloped as I tried to think of an answer.

He stepped closer, and I instinctively stepped back until I hit a wall. Our eyes locked onto one another until I broke our gaze, but he lifted my chin, which made me suck in a deep breath. My heart thundered as Tristan leaned forward and tugged my chin closer. Right when our lips were about to touch, he paused and whispered, "Is this okay?"

I nodded, fighting the lightheadedness that engulfed me from holding my breath for so long. When I couldn't take it anymore, I grabbed the back of his head and opened my mouth fully to take him in. I felt his tongue invade my mouth and our heavy breaths filled my ears. He wrapped his arms around my waist and pulled me closer as if he could meld our bodies together. I held his face between my hands and kissed him like it was my first time. I didn't remember this fiery feeling igniting in my belly last time I kissed a boy. This felt like an inferno only Tristan could quench. It kept spreading lower until it caused an ache between my legs. We kissed like we didn't need air to breathe. We kept pushing our bodies closer to each other, and our hands ran down each other's backs as if we needed it to put out the flame that ignited inside of us.

Tristan traced kisses on my jaw and down my neck. I clenched my thighs together as the heat intensified. He lifted my legs up and propped my weight against the wall, then rubbed his hard erection perfectly where I needed him to ease the burning pain. *Oh god. Yes.* A loud moan escaped my mouth before my heavy breathing resumed. Tristan continued to rub our hips together and was about to capture my mouth once again, but then we heard the loud bang of a door. We both froze and looked in the noise's direction and saw the retreating back of Sebastian.

I scrambled out of Tristan's arms and stepped away to give us some distance apart. I didn't know why I felt guilty, but I didn't want to make things worse with Sebastian. Plus, I didn't know what came over me. I almost had sex with a guy I barely knew in a classroom. Without another look at Tristan, I once again ran out of the room. This time he let me go.

Once my heart settled into a more regular rhythm, I slowed down my pace and went straight to the library and registered for my classes. It took me thirty minutes to decide which classes to take. I finally just picked introductory courses that I thought were interesting, like Humanities, Psychology, and Sociology. Then, I settled into the library seat and started on the classwork. I had the option to do it back in my room, but I didn't want to run into Tristan. So, I hid out in the library and stayed as late as possible. I even skipped lunch. I knew I couldn't skip dinner, so I went straight to the cafeteria as soon as it opened, hoping it would be empty and most of the students would still be in class.

My heart sank when I saw the princes sitting in their usual spot in the cafeteria. Tristan waved me over as soon as he spotted me. I glanced at Sebastian, and as usual, he acted like I didn't exist. I waved back and pointed to the buffet.

Moving slowly and taking as much time as I could in getting my food, I hoped that Shay or Lori would show up so I would have an excuse not to sit with the princes. Unfortunately, they didn't show, so I walked to their table filled with apprehension.

"Hey. How was the independent study?" Tristan asked.

My eyebrows rose and gestured to their empty plates. "I don't want to interrupt. I'm fine eating alone."

Sebastian snorted but said nothing.

"Don't be silly." Tristan grabbed a fry from my plate and smirked.

I tried not to smile, to not encourage him, but my face burned as he held my gaze and my eyes darted to his lips, my imagination taking me back to the kiss we shared earlier.

"Oh, for god's sake. Stop it!" Sebastian snarled.

My eyes grew wide, taken aback by his sudden outburst. "What's your problem?"

He got up with a loud scrape of his chair and leaned down close enough that I could see the flecks of brown and gold in his grey-blue eyes. "You're the problem. Ever since you got here, you've been a mess, and you're dragging us down with you." I felt his breath on my face then he gave me a disdainful look, before pushing off the table and marching out of the cafeteria.

I gaped at his retreating back in disbelief, then I noticed the other students gawking and whispering. I turned and took in a shaky breath as I stared at my untouched sandwich while I struggled to keep my unshed tears at bay.

"Hey, are you okay? Ignore him. He's just..." He placed a hand on my shoulder, which I shrugged off.

"I'm fine." I blinked away the tears from my eyes and forced a smile.

Tristan kept eyeing me as we sat in an awkward silence. My chest felt heavy from Sebastian's words, which irritated me because I shouldn't care what Sebastian thought of me. He'd been rude to me since I got here. Yeah, I saw a glimmer of kindness from him the other night, but obviously, he was suffering from a split personality. I shouldn't have to take that crap from him.

Tristan gently pulled the sandwich from my grip and flashed me one of his disarming smiles. "The poor sandwich did nothing to you. If you won't eat it, I'll take it. It's a crime to waste perfectly good food."

I raised my eyebrows and looked at the empty stack of plates in front of him.

He shrugged. "I'm a growing wolf. I need my calories," he said in between bites.

I chuckled, and just like that, I felt lighter. Tristan really has a knack for making me feel better. "Are you taking any independent studies?"

"Yes, Seb and I are required to know about business and politics. Uncle Rahl insisted we needed to be ready to take over when needed. He owns a lot of businesses around the city, and he deals with the human government. It's all boring stuff if you ask me."

"Yeah. Well, at least you know what to take. I don't really know what I want to do, so I just took many minor subjects. The introductions were pretty boring, and I'm nowhere close to figuring out what I want to do when I graduate."

"What were your plans before all of this?"

I looked down as I remembered how excited Mom was that I was going to college. I realized that Tristan was still waiting for my answer, so I forced a smile and said, "My mom and I were so focused on getting me to college, we really didn't plan that far ahead. I guess a part of us didn't really believe I would make it to college. Or we didn't want to jinx it. We just wanted to afford it. When I applied for a scholarship, my grades and SAT's were great, but I didn't declare a major. Even then, I wasn't hopeful that I would actually go to college. When I got my acceptance, we planned the trip right away, and we didn't really have time to talk about it." I glanced down at my soggy fries, and I picked one up and chewed the end. "The last thing my mom and I talked about was that she was going to sell the house, and we were going to rent an apartment closer to college." Guilt and longing hit me since this was the first time I'd really thought of my mom since I got here. I wish she was here. This time a tear escaped and fell down my cheek. I reached up to brush it off, but Tristan beat me to it. We gazed at each other for a moment before he tugged on my hand and said, "Let's get out of here."

"Where are we going?"

"I want to show you something." We walked in silence as Tristan held my hand, which I was getting used to.

We kept climbing up the stairs, and every time I asked, he just shook his head. I didn't realize how out of shape I was until about half way up and I had to stop and catch my breath...

"I've never seen a Shifter out of breath before," Tristan teased.

"Shut up," I said in between heavy breaths.

"Maybe you should actually eat more."

"It's not normal to walk ten flights of stairs and not get winded," I complained.

"Um... It is for a Shifter."

I rolled my eyes and gestured for him to continue.

"Do you want me to carry you? You look like you're about to pass out. This was supposed to be a romantic gesture." He frowned.

I continued to gesture for him to keep walking since I was still too out of breath to talk.

He cocked a brow, and in one swoop, I was over his shoulder, bouncing as he took the stairs two at a time.

"Tristan," I said in between breaths as I weakly smacked his ass. "Put me down."

I attempted to wiggle out of his hold but eventually gave up. The bastard was freaking sprinting up the stairs two at a time with me on his shoulders. He wasn't even breathing hard. Show off.

Finally, after a few more flights of stairs, he kicked open a door and dropped me to the ground gently. He flashed me a grin which was damn cute.

"How are you not tired?" He didn't even break a damn sweat.

His brow scrunched. "Shifter?"

"Well, I'm a Shifter too, but those damn stairs almost killed me. Wasn't there an elevator or something?"

He chuckled. "You sound so human." He tugged on my hand, and we walked on what looked like the flat roof of the main building. I looked over the brick wall, and my eyes grew wide as I took in the view of the grounds from up here. Thick trees and green grass as far as the eye could see surrounded the academy. The three towers peeked through the dense vegetation. It looked so peaceful. *How could this place exist in the middle of a city?*

"Wow, this is..."

"Do you like it?"

"This is amazing! This view is better than the city," I said in awe. I ran to all sides to check the view. "Did you know, in the country, the highest building we had was only four stories? And we didn't have land this green! We had large farmlands but never just grass and thick forest trees."

He chuckled. "I'm glad you like it."

I gazed at his green eyes, and his thick lips which were pulled into a bright smile. He was so beautiful. I noticed his adam's apple bob up and down, and his smile wavered.

"How did you know?" I whispered.

"Know what?" His eyes narrowed in confusion.

"That I loved heights."

"I didn't. I wanted to share my favorite place in the academy with you," he said, his eyes shifting to the side.

Was he embarrassed? Could he be more adorable?

I reached for his face and stood on my tiptoes to reach his mouth. He grabbed my hips, and we shared a soft and slow kiss. Our lips danced as if we wanted to savor every moment. It wasn't like our first kiss, where we couldn't get enough of each other. This kiss was slow and sensual but was just as intoxicating as the last. Our tongues caressed each other like they were tasting the best dessert and couldn't get enough of it. I felt lightheaded from our kiss, most likely because I needed to breathe, but I didn't want to detach from Tristan's mouth. Finally, I sucked in a deep breath, and he slowly kissed and nipped my neck down to my collarbone. He made his way to the other side of my neck agonizingly slowly.

My god, could someone die from pleasure? I felt like he was torturing me and pleasuring me at the same time. The feeling was too intense, but I didn't want him to stop.

"Tristan," I breathed.

"Yes, baby. Tell me what you want," he said as he kissed between my breasts. His thumb brushed my nipple, which sent electricity down my spine. I jerked and felt my knees buckle. Tristan's powerful arms wrapped around my waist and captured my mouth once again as he walked us to the wall. He took off my blazer and, with shaking fingers, untucked my shirt from my skirt and unbuttoned it until my breasts were bare for him to see. I'd never had a boy reach second base before, and right now, Tristan gaped at my opened shirt with my lacy bra barely covering my breasts. I hunched my shoulders to hide from him, which he noticed.

"Why are you trying to hide from me? You're fucking gorgeous," he breathed.

I shook my head and forced my arms to stay at my side, even if I wanted to cross them over my chest.

He frowned. "Are we moving too fast? I know we're moving too fast, but Vi, you're driving me fucking crazy. Even my wolf is restless. He wants to be around you twenty-four seven. I know it sounds cliche, but I've never felt this way over anyone before. Please let me know if we're going too fast. We'll go at your pace. I don't care. I just want to be with you."

I wrapped my arms around my chest and frowned. "It's not that. I just..." I turned and looked over the wall once again to gather my thoughts to best explain that I'd never been with a man before.

Tristan caged me with his arms, and I felt his desire on my back. I clenched my thighs to ease the ache as if it responded to his. "I don't mind waiting, Vi."

"We don't really know each other. What if this isn't real? Professor Wilkins said we must get together to ensure the alpha line continues. What if we're just responding to those desires?"

"Does it matter? What we feel is genuine enough. I feel it. It's strong, and I'm certain it will not fade. It would make sense if we were mates. That's the strongest bond a Shifter can ever have. It's supposed to be strong and instant. It defies logic. Is it magic or fate or destiny that makes us have these feelings for each other? I don't care. It's as real as anything. Mates are forever, and the bond is unbreakable. They are rare and sacred."

His words touched me, and hope sparked inside of me. I twisted to look into his eyes. "Do you think I'm your mate?" I whispered.

"Yes," he said with certainty. "My wolf is restless when you're not around. From the moment I saw you, my focus shifted to you like suddenly you were the center of my universe."

"Wait. That's too heavy. We don't really know each other. If we're really mates, as you say, does that mean we don't have a say in the bond?"

"I don't know. I just know how I feel."

"But I don't feel what you're describing." I frowned. I wanted to feel what he felt, but I didn't. If he were indeed my mate, then I wouldn't be alone.

He stepped back. My head snapped in his direction, and I caught the hurt that crossed his eyes.

"You mean you don't feel the bond?"

"I don't feel my wolf, so I don't feel what you're describing. However, I feel this strong desire, which clouds my judgment. I barely know you, and already I've almost given up my virginity to you. Twice!"

"What did you say?" His eyes grew wide.

My hand flew to my mouth. Oh my god, I didn't mean to blurt it out like that. I felt my face burn, so I covered my face in embarrassment.

"Viola, look at me." I slowly lowered my hands. "Are you telling me you're a virgin?"

I nodded.

"How is that possible? How old are you?"

I crossed my arms and scowled. "Eighteen. That's not unheard of! Not everyone loses their virginity in high school, you know!"

"No. I didn't mean that. Supernaturals are highly sexual creatures. We have too much energy coursing through us we need to expel, plus births in supernaturals are not rare per se but much less common than humans, so I don't know. We're more wired to want to procreate?" He smirked.

I rolled my eyes.

"I'm serious. We don't have birth control. We consider any pregnancies a blessing since it's not that common. Only one in ten couples get pregnant, so we cherish infants."

"Seriously?"

"Maybe it's the universe trying to keep the balance. Otherwise, we would easily defeat the humans. We're stronger and more powerful. The only advantage they have over us is numbers." He picked up my blazer and helped me put it on.

"We'll take it at your own pace, okay? You know what I want. I'm not going anywhere."

I nodded, and he leaned in and brushed his lips against mine. He leaned his forehead to mine, and we stayed still for a moment, just enjoying the promise and the possibilities.

"Let's get out of here before I do something I regret." He grabbed my hand and led me to the door.

He eyed the stairs and swept me off my feet, then carried me all the way down.

We got down the stairs in no time. Shifter strength was impressive.

"Why do you think I don't have the same strength and stamina?"

He shrugged. "You're definitely different." He eyed me sideways and placed his arms around me. "Don't worry, we'll figure out where you came from."

I hoped so. I really wanted to know why I was so different from everyone. I also would like to know if there was a possibility that Tristan was my mate. The thought of it made my heart race. *What would Sebastian think of us being mates if he found out?* Annoyed with myself, I dismissed the nagging thought. I didn't know why I was thinking about Sebastian. If I were honest with myself, I really wanted Tristan to be my mate. The thought brought comfort to me.

Chapter 7

I couldn't believe I'd been in school for several weeks. I'd even fallen into a daily routine with Shay and Lori, where we met up at breakfast and alternated eating lunch with the princes. Sebastian had changed little. He tolerated my presence but hardly said a word to me, which was a vast improvement from the hurtful words he flung at me that one day.

"Pay attention, Viola," Carlisle said.

My head turned from my outstretched palms and I glared at him. "What do you think I'm doing?" I snapped. "I can't produce magic."

"We know you can. You did it before. Try again. Close your eyes and feel for the magic inside of you. Once you feel it, think of what you want to happen and do it. If it helps, move your hands and wave them around to help channel the energy."

He might as well be speaking Latin because he made little sense. I felt nothing. There was no magic inside of me.

"You're not trying hard enough," he bit out.

I gritted my teeth and let out a loud huff through my nose, while gesturing wildly with my hands. "You sho..." I threw him across the room, and his back hit the wall. "Oh my god! Are you okay?"

He groaned and sat up. "That's what I'm talking about. Maybe next time, don't direct it at me?" He smiled, but blood started dripping from his cut lip.

I grabbed a tissue and pressed it on his mouth. He froze, and for a moment, we held each other's eyes. My heart skipped a beat. I cleared my throat and directed my attention to the cut, which had stopped bleeding.

"Are you ready to try again?" he asked.

I nodded, avoiding his eyes. We tried for the rest of the period with no success, which persisted every time we met. The only time I would see a hint of my powers was when he used his, but all I could do is copy what he did, which wasn't much progress since we couldn't move forward until I could call powers on my own.

I'd had no contact with Kol. I'd been keeping an eye out for him, but I hadn't seen him around. I supposed he'd changed his mind about helping me. When I saw him with his crew, he avoided my eyes and pretended I didn't exist while the rest of the Vampires left me alone.

At the most, I would sometimes catch them throwing me a nasty look when they thought I couldn't see them. The witches were more obvious with their disdain. When I passed by, they would put their heads together and loudly whisper "freak" or "whore" or other nasty things I ignored. The Shifters were friendly but kept their distance.

Tristan and I had been spending a lot of time together but had avoided being alone too often since we couldn't seem to keep our hands off each other. It was getting harder each day to hold back. What was I waiting for? Some kind of sign?

Tristan was amazing and attentive and the best boyfriend a girl could ask for. That's right—boyfriend—something I'd never really had before. The label still made my heart flutter. But Tristan had definitely made it clear since the beginning that he wanted everyone to know we were together—he was possessive like that. He growled at anyone who looked my way, and he hated Kol and Carlisle. I thought Tristan might be jealous of them. I assured him he had nothing to worry about, although a small part of me couldn't deny the connection I felt for the two...well, three if you counted Sebastian, who made it clear he wanted nothing to do with me.

Stretching my limbs, I laid in bed, enjoying a lazy morning. It was the weekend, and for once, I didn't have to get up butt-crack early. I had no plans for today, and I didn't have to be anywhere. I'd stolen some fruits and granola bar from the cafeteria, so I was set for breakfast.

Waking up naturally instead of using a blaring, loud alarm clock put me in a great mood. I savored the feeling of waking up refreshed.

The clock read nine-thirty. I was contemplating what I wanted to do for the day when there was a loud knock on the door. I groaned and hoped that whoever it was would give up and go away.

I could hear persistent knocking even over the pillow on top of my head.

Can't a girl enjoy her moment of peace? I padded to the door and opened it with a frown.

"Good morning, sleepyhead." Tristan beamed.

I rolled my eyes and marched back to bed.

"I take it you're not a morning person? I brought breakfast."

"Tristan, this is the first time I've gotten to sleep in. Go away," I threw over my shoulder.

Ignoring me, he hopped on the other side of the bed and stared.

"Stop it." I flipped to the other side, and I heard his soft intake of breath.

Wha...oh yeah, I remembered I wore a thin camisole and lace bikini panties to bed, which showed half of my ass. I froze. I was reasonably sure he wasn't breathing until finally, I felt his weight shift. He moved closer, and I felt his hard length against my back while his hand rested on my hip.

"Vi, you're too fucking enticing. You need to tell me to stop because I only have so much self-control," he whispered. His lips touched the lobe of my ear as his breath caressed my neck, which caused my skin to prickle.

His hand slid to my stomach then he pulled me closer, which brought me flush against his erection. My heart raced in my chest as he ran his fingers on my thigh and licked and nipped my shoulder. I reached for his head and captured his mouth as my breathing became more labored. Soon he was on top of me and was grinding his hard length over the thin, lacy fabric of my panties. The intense sensation had me gasping in his mouth. "Baby, tell me you've had an orgasm before?"

I shook my head.

"You mean you don't touch yourself?" He pulled away and stared at me in disbelief.

My face flushed, but my foggy brain was too slow to give an explanation.

"Baby, I'm gonna own a lot of your firsts," he said huskily as he continued to rock against me.

He took my camisole off and stared at my breasts. "So fucking gorgeous," he murmured. My eyes closed from the sensation as his hand massaged my breasts, then his mouth replaced his hands. In no time, he had my back arching and me crying out, "Tristan!" It was too much, but also, I couldn't get enough. He'd awoken an animalistic desire in me.

With a ragged breath, I pulled his mouth to mine and kissed him hungrily and tore the shirt off his chest. Unable to get enough, my nails raked against his skin as my hands roamed his firm muscles, and my hips rocked with him, trying to chase away the heat that built below my stomach. "Fuck, baby. If you continue to do that, I won't be able to stop."

"Who says I want you to stop?" I breathed.

He looked deep into my eyes. "Are you sure that's what you want? I don't want you to regret your first time."

"Shut up and kiss me, Tristan." If my words weren't clear enough, my shaky fingers unbuttoning his jeans should do it. He took over and kicked off his pants and underwear. I reached between his thighs and silenced his groan with a kiss. I ran my hand up and down his thick, hard length.

His hand gripped my ass, his nails leaving pleasurable indentations on my skin, and then his breathing came in short bursts. He slipped my panties to the side. "Fuck, so wet and ready."

Fuck! This time I might have drawn blood on his back as he elicited foreign sensations in me. He stopped, which made my eyes open. I groaned in frustration; I needed him to finish what he started and ease off this raging inferno he teased inside of me. But then, I watched him get in between my legs, take off my panties, and replace his fingers with his mouth. My eyes grew wide, and I threw my head back as I completely lost it. He had to hold me down as I bucked from the intensity. The inferno peaked. Then soon, he had me calling out his name and quivering from my release. "Holy fuck," I breathed as I felt myself come down from the high.

However, I felt Tristan slowly enter me. My eyes flew open as the combination of pain mixed with pleasure hit me. We gazed into each other's eyes as he fully settled inside of me. We both gasped. Then, I felt his wolf, and I was confident he could feel mine. As our wolves connected, our souls danced, and my pleasure doubled. My nerve endings were on fire. I could feel his emotions, which intensified my own.

Tristan's slow pace got faster, and as I felt our bodies slide into each other, and the need for a release grew. His eyes glowed brighter, and his wolf stared at me from behind his eyes. The sensation kept growing, and I gripped his arms tightly, calling out his name as I rode out the burst of orgasm. I felt his fangs dig into my shoulder as I felt his release join mine.

Tristan rolled to the side as we were getting our racing hearts back to normal. I turned to face him but paused.

"What is it? Are you okay?" He pulled me close and trailed his fingers up and down my hip.

What was that? I frowned in confusion as I still felt Tristan's wolf.

Yes, we're bonded now. We can feel each other's wolves.

I sat up abruptly. "Did you just speak inside my head and read my thoughts?" That won't do. I couldn't have anyone inside my head.

"Baby, we're bonded. We can feel each other and speak with each other through our link, but don't freak. I can only read what you're sending out."

How the hell should I know what I'm sending out?

His lips turned up, and he pressed his thumb on my furrowed brow. "You need to shield."

I opened my mouth to ask what he was talking about when he continued. "Close your eyes and picture something solid surrounding your thoughts."

Raising a brow, I studied him for a moment, then closed my eyes. I pictured a concrete wall surrounding my brain. It wasn't easy. I didn't know how to depict thoughts, so eventually, I imagined an enclosed, solid steel box.

"Good. Now only let out stuff you want me to read. Like, picture a window or a door."

That didn't sound easy. I lost concentration each time I tried, so it took us all morning to practice.

"You're doing great. Now, just picture putting the box away on a shelf or a drawer or something and forget about it. Only take it out if you need to communicate with me."

It took me another hour to do as he asked since I couldn't really make myself just forget. However, eventually, as he successfully distracted me with another round of sex, I realized I could access the box whenever I wanted.

Tristan had to drag me to the cafeteria for dinner since we skipped breakfast and lunch. I could have stayed in bed, but it was essential to keep up his sustenance. He had been visibly more tired by late afternoon. "I don't see why I had to go with you. You should spend time with Sebastian." I slowed my walk and dragged my feet.

"You need to eat as well, and you two need to get along, eventually." He tugged on my hand. "I promise, I'll make it worth your while when we get back to our room." Not missing his innuendo, a smile formed on my lips.

I didn't know how much I was missing until I finally slept with Tristan. Now, I felt complete. Our bond had brought our encounters to another level. We could communicate in our thoughts more efficiently than words, so we knew what each other liked. We both dropped our barriers when we had sex, which intensified our intimacy.

"What the fuck!"

We turned to Sebastian, whose eyes glowed and fists clenched on his sides. "Tell me you two didn't. Tris..." His nose flared as he glared at Tristan and me.

I avoided his eyes, guilt filling in my stomach. Why did I feel guilty? We weren't together.

"Seb, brother. Let me explain." Tristan took a step closer to Sebastian, but he growled and flashed his fangs. I tugged at Tristan to my side, and anger surfaced.

"What is your problem, Sebastian?"

His fur rippled on his arms, and a roar escaped his elongating snout until finally, a giant wolf stood before us. The wolf growled at mine and Tristan's joined hands, and right before he spun to run away, he caught my eyes, and I saw pain. It confused me. Did he think I was stealing Tristan from him?

"That wasn't how I planned for him to find out," Tristan said with his head bowed.

"Should you go after him?"

He shook his head. "No, he needs to cool off. I'll talk to him when he's ready."

Both Tristan and I were quiet as we ate our dinner. I didn't know why I worried so much about Sebastian's feelings. He'd been nothing but an ass to me since I got here. However, I could tell that Tristan was troubled about hurting his brother.

He didn't smile or say much, and he only had a couple of plates instead of several. Shortly after we finished eating, he dropped me off at my room and said he needed to find Sebastian.

I didn't see him for the rest of the weekend, which had my brain going in different directions. What if they fought and injured each other, or what if Tristan changed his mind? What if Sebastian hated me more now? That thought really bugged me. I didn't understand why I cared so much about Sebastian. I almost reached out a few times through our bond, but I didn't want to look desperate or clingy, so by Sunday night, I needed to get out of my room. I spent the entire day stressing over what happened between the two of them that I needed a break from it all.

Sitting in the library, I pulled up the assigned work for my independent studies for the week. I figured I could get ahead. I needed the distraction, and also, my room had started feeling claustrophobic. Not wanting to bother Shay and Lori, I ended up here. I looked around, surprised to see half of the tables occupied with students. As usual, I ignored the glares and whispers thrown my way. I sat in my corner, minding my own business, reading about the six major psychological theories, when I felt the hairs on the back of my neck stand up quickly, followed by the peppering of goosebumps on my skin. I felt negative energy attack me. I looked around and found two female Casters with their heads bowed together. They didn't look familiar to me, but then again, I ignored everyone outside of my circle. One of them glanced in my direction but quickly averted her eyes. I gathered my belongings and swung my bag on my shoulder, then made my way to them. One of them hid something quickly under the desk as I approached. They still had their heads bowed close together as I placed my hands on their backs and lowered my head close to their ears.

"You don't know who you're fucking with. Don't say I didn't warn you," I hissed and stood straight. Their heads snapped to me with hatred in their eyes.

I turned and left the library, hoping that my warning and reputation were enough to stop the attempts. Didn't they know it was for their own good to just leave me alone? Who knew what my weird power would do to them? I had been trying to keep my head bowed and mind my business. Why didn't they just leave me alone?

Chapter 8

My anxiety over the weekend had been for nothing. Monday at breakfast came, and Tristan made a beeline to me, followed by Sebastian. I kept shooting glances at them, but they acted as though nothing had happened. Tristan held my hand, but he'd definitely toned down the flirting. Not wanting to stir the pot since Sebastian didn't glare at me in hostility, which I called progress, I played along and acted like the weekend never happened. Sometimes, I caught Tristan's stare, and his caress lingered, but it was gone before I was sure.

"We don't have Shifter class today," Shay said as she pushed her plate away.

"Why?" I asked, already done with my meal.

"Some last-minute assembly. There are some important announcements," Lori said.

"Usually, when they have an assembly, we also skip the second period, so our next class is combat," Tristan absently said while playing with my hand.

"Shoot. I need to turn in my late paper to Professor Taylor. Save me a seat. I'll see you guys there," I called before anyone could say anything. I ran to the classroom, hoping to catch him, but he wasn't there, so I went to the staff lounge but right as I turned the corner, I felt someone hit the back of my head. My vision darkened and the world spun. I was unsure if I passed out, but when my head cleared, there was a sack over my head, and someone had tied my arms behind my back. I struggled against my bindings and tried to scream, but they had gagged me as well. Someone slapped me across the face. "Stupid fucking bitch. You'll pay for that."

"Hurry! What's taking so long?"

The hit had my ears ringing, so I couldn't make out the voices.

"It's not working."

"What are you doing, you freak!" Whack! Another hit, this time a punch on my cheek, which had me falling backward from the chair. I hit my head, which made me dizzy again.

I heard a commotion and the scraping of furniture against the floor. I feared they were coming to do more harm, so I curled against myself and tensed for more blows. Instead, I felt gentle arms pick me up as we sped out of the room. Every step left my bruised body in pain, so I didn't struggle. I waited to see if this person wanted to do me more harm. I was set gently down on a cold, wooden table in no time, and the person removed the sack on my head. I blinked my swollen eyes open and saw Sebastian in front of me, wearing an expression of concern, an underlying fury in his tense face. He took off my gag next, and I spat out some blood. Then he took off my bindings and massaged my hands. "Are you okay?" His voice was gentle. "Of course you're not okay. Look at you." He clenched his jaw as his gentle hands prodded my face, which made me flinch in pain.

"I'm sorry. How are you feeling? Are you dizzy? Why aren't you healing as fast?"

I shook my head, which made everything spin. He caught me and held me until I stopped seeing spots. His touch helped ease the aches and pains my body was protesting to.

"Talk to me, Vi."

"Give me a moment." I didn't move from his embrace.

In response, he settled next to me and held me quietly as he brushed my hair with his fingers. It felt soothing and had my eyes feeling heavy. I didn't know how long we stayed in that position. I must have dozed off for a bit. When I stirred, his arms tightened around me.

"What happened?" I croaked and met his eyes.

He studied my face, and after a moment, he looked relieved. "I'm glad your healing abilities finally kicked in. You heal slowly for a Shifter." He tucked a hair behind my ear and held my gaze captured.

"I almost died twice tonight when I thought I lost you," he whispered as his hand cupped my face.

I froze at his words and his expression; his emotions clear in his eyes. Sebastian had never looked at me with tenderness before. It was always with annoyance and loathing. The way he looked at me now had my heart racing. Like I was important to him. "Don't scare me like that again, Vi." His tone was commanding and possessive.

I made a noise in my throat, but no words would come out. Sebastian looked at me like he owned me, but not like I was a possession. He looked at me like I was the thing he cherished most of all and that he couldn't live without. I opened my mouth in another attempt to say something, but his mouth crashed into mine. The tension between us that had been brewing since day one came crashing down. The fire inside of me ignited instantaneously. I met his bruising kiss stroke per stroke. Thank goodness for quick healing; I felt back to normal. Otherwise, I wouldn't be able to handle the way

Sebastian grabbed at me roughly. He ripped my shirt off, then my bra, and soon his teeth nipped at my nipples in a painful but pleasurable way. I couldn't recall how his shirt came off, but I felt his defined muscles as I clawed at them. He laid me on the table and took my jeans off and thrust into me in one smooth motion. I cried out in both pain and pleasure. Sebastian wasn't gentle. He roughly thrust in and out of me as he controlled my hip movement. Every time he moved, I cried out in pleasure as he was hitting a sensitive spot. My orgasm spasmed out of me quickly. Sebastian grunted as I squeezed him tightly. He flipped me over the desk, which felt deeper. He then added a thumb on my nub, which had a scream building in my chest. When I felt another release, he bit me on the other shoulder, opposite from where Tristan bit, and then followed with his orgasm. I laid on the desk unmoving. These two princes were going to be the death of me. Sebastian trailed kisses down my back gently, which had me squirming, then I felt him nudge my legs apart. I tried to look behind me, wondering what he was doing. But he kept a firm hand on my lower back, which kept me pinned on the desk. Then I felt his tongue lick my center. My legs jerked as he quickly had me cresting close to another orgasm. He thrust three fingers in me, and another wave of release escaped me. Before I had recovered, he pulled me onto his lap, and I gently sunk onto his shaft. This time, he went slowly, and we held each other's gaze. It was intimate. He kissed me gently, and when he looked into my eyes, his wolf was looking at me. We could no longer go slow as our wolves' addition had our bodies sizzling with heat. Soon we both rode a long wave of another release. Sebastian bit me again.

What's with the biting?

I like your taste, mate.

Does that mean we're bonded as well as Tristan?

Yes. You are my bonded mate. I felt his thoughts and emotions as he opened up his shields.

I felt his uncertainty and jealousy, so I dropped my shields to show him what I felt. I didn't prefer one prince over the other. They were both my mates. However, it still didn't take away my confusion.

The amusement in his thoughts had me frowning. *It's not unheard of for a female alpha to have several mates. If you think about it, it's a safety measure to ensure our species don't go extinct.*

Then why were you upset when you first found out about Tristan and me?

I was jealous. I'm a prick. Can you forgive me? He rocked his hips. We hadn't moved even though he was no longer hard.

"Is that why you were such an asshole to me?"

He captured my mouth instead of answering, and I felt him twitch inside of me. "Yes. Forgive me. I didn't like the idea of sharing my mate, so I fought the pull you had on me," he said, rocking us gently. His movement elicited warmth in me. "I didn't think I had a chance after how I acted."

His movement grew faster as I felt his hard length thrust in and out of me. "There was definitely a pull towards you, but I thought you hated me," I said, breathing hard.

"Are you upset that I bonded us too quickly?" he questioned, slowing down.

I pulled his face to mine and took over as I rocked us harder and faster. "No. I want to be mated with both of you. It feels right," I grunted as I felt another round of orgasm build.

He reached between us and rubbed my center, and soon I was gone. He soon followed. Afterwards, we got dressed.

I was grateful to have him by my side. Otherwise, I would lose it. He made me feel safe. He and Tristan were a reminder to never give up and to fight. It was easy to just hide in the corner and rock myself with self-pity, wishing to join my parents. I'd often felt that way when I first lost my mom, but the princes give me a reason to fight and see another day. Sometimes, that was all you needed—a reminder.

I paused in zipping his jacket, which he gave to me in place of my shirt that he ripped. "Where's Tristan?"

"He dealt with the assholes." His jaw clenched. "I hope he killed all of them. If he didn't, I will," he growled.

I laid a hand on his chest, and he soon calmed. Then I reached out to Tristan through our bond.

I'm fine. Enjoy your time with Sebastian. We'll talk later, he said, which had me sighing. I knew that Tristan was safe, and he didn't seem to mind my bond with Sebastian.

"Tris is in our room waiting for you whenever you're ready to head back. We can stay here as long as you want," Sebastian said.

I looked around for the first time and noticed that we were in an abandoned concrete room. There was some dusty furniture in the corner and a barred window on one side, as well as a heavy door. We were in the center of the room on a large oak desk. "Where are we?"

"An abandoned room at the back of the castle. Tris and I stumbled into it one night as we ran through the woods. We cleaned it up and placed a lock on the door. We found it by accident. Otherwise, it's hidden and hard to find. We kept it just in case we needed an escape or to lie low." The room had a couple of lamps on the wall that emitted low lights, but otherwise, it was empty.

"Are you okay? I know your wounds have healed, but are you okay?"

Tears pricked in my eyes, but I didn't let them flow. I nodded. I'd be fine as long as I had my mates with me. These fuckers kept trying to bring me down, but they were just strengthening me. Payback would be a bitch.

"If you want to head back, Tris is waiting, and we can talk about it."

I wrapped my arms around Sebastian and sighed in comfort. We stayed for a moment in each other's arms, and I basked in the security my mate brought until I was ready to face what had happened.

WE WALKED INTO TRISTAN'S room, hand in hand, but paused as we found Rahl, Mr. Wilson, Kol, and Carlisle. I ran to Rahl, and he gave me a fierce hug. "Are you okay?" He pulled away and inspected me closely.

I blinked back the tears as the emotions threatened to break. I needed him. I was glad he was here. If I didn't get to have my parents, I was glad that I had Rahl. "Yes. What are you doing here?" He was like a second father to me, and I hadn't seen him in months.

He frowned, and then his eyes narrowed on Sebastian, then me, and then his gaze bounced back to Tristan. "We will address important matters first, then the four of us will speak," he said to us.

Does he know?

Yes, they both said at the same time with a resigned tone.

Wait. The three of us can communicate at the same time? Can you both communicate?

Yes, Tristan said.

We'll tell you more later when others are not around. He looked at the other three in the room and stood behind my chair.

"Vi, can you please tell us what happened?" Rahl asked.

I racked my brain for a moment, then whispered, "I don't know. I didn't see or hear much. One minute I was running towards the staff room, then the next, my vision got dark. Then when I woke up, I was gagged, bound, and there was a sack over my head. I heard them fighting. There were several of them, male and female. I couldn't make them out because someone kept hitting me, so I couldn't hear very well. Then the next thing I knew, Seb rescued me." I had my fingers twisted together and looked up gratefully at Sebastian. He grabbed my hand and squeezed. "How did you find me?"

"Tristan and I followed when you took off, but you were fast and had a lead on us, and we didn't know where you were going, so it took us a minute to find you."

"They had a Caster working with them because we were less than five minutes behind when we lost her scent close to the staff lounge. They were masking her scent." Sebastian glared at Carlisle.

Carlisle straightened in his seat, and his eyes darkened.

"When we got to her, a group of Casters and Vampires surrounded her. We weren't sure what they were trying to accomplish, but whatever it was failed. They looked worse for wear even before I was done with them," Tristan said darkly.

"I will personally guarantee that those involved will not go unpunished," Kol bit out.

Were they angry on my behalf, or were they mad for their kin? I looked at the dean, whose expression was blank, and Kol, who held a severe expression. If it wasn't for the tensing of his shoulders, I wouldn't have thought that he was upset. "Where are they now?" He turned to Mr. Wilson.

"They have been apprehended and are locked in their rooms," he replied.

"I will need to speak with them," Rahl said in an almost growl.

"With all due respect, sir. I don't think that's a good idea." Carlisle shifted in his seat and lowered his gaze. A sign of respect.

Rahl's brows drew together.

"If one royal gets involved, then it's just a matter of time before the others follow. Wouldn't it be best if we kept this within the academy?" Carlisle turned to Mr. Wilson, asking for backup.

He shook his head regretfully. "That's why I'm here. It's too late for that. The coven has caught wind of what happened last night and about the incident on Sunday, and they are on their way. It was just fortunate that my informant warned me of the plans." He leaned forward with a troubled look.

Did he say Sunday? I racked my brains about what he referred to but drew a blank.

"What happened on Sunday?" Tristan asked.

I looked around the room, but they all wore a confused expression, so no one knew what he was referring to.

Rahl looked at me and asked, "Vi, can you tell us what happened on Sunday?" For a minute, my heart raced, thinking he was asking about my bonding with Tristan, but that happened on Saturday. What happened on... My head snapped in Rahl's direction. "Wait. Are you referring to the two Casters in the library?"

"What Casters?" Carlisle asked.

"What happened?" Tristan asked.

"Why didn't you tell us?" Sebastian said.

I glanced at each one, then rested my gaze on Kol since he was the only one who didn't speak—his expression unreadable. Then I answered, "I was studying in the library when I felt an attack. I saw two female Casters, and I warned them not to fuck with me. That's all." I shrugged.

Rahl studied me for a moment. "Did anything else happen?"

I shook my head.

"Can you tell us exactly what happened? In detail," Rahl insisted.

What the hell happened? Why was he making a big deal? I trusted him, so I told the room everything that transpired down to what I felt and my actions that night.

"Wait. You felt an attack, but nothing happened?" Carlisle asked.

I shrugged. "I don't think so. At least, I noticed nothing."

"Who attacked her?" Mr. Wilson asked.

"The Lieberman girl and Conrad," Rahl said, his eyes still focused on me.

"Are you sure you felt nothing? We know those two girls for their powerful curses." Mr. Wilson peered at me as if he was looking for the curse.

I shook my head while I thought hard about if there was something off. Nope. I felt perfectly fine.

"The reason the coven caught wind of the incident is that the girl's curse backfired. They both combined their powers to power the curse, and then they both came down with open sores that won't heal."

Those bitches wanted to hit me with that? Serves them right!

"That's not the worse part."

"There's more?" Tristan asked in an incredulous voice. I was glad that he was by my side since he seemed to voice what I couldn't.

"Their parents got involved, not because of a failed spell, but because they lost their powers."

"What do you mean they lost their powers?" Mr. Wilson asked.

"This has been kept within the coven, but they can no longer cast. The most they can do is a simple spell, but even with those, they have difficulty," Rahl said.

"How is that possible?" Carlisle asked, looking around the room, hoping for answers. That news clearly disturbed him.

"I see why the coven wanted to get involved. This is serious." Mr. Wilson murmured.

"I don't understand. Did they try to take away my powers, and it backfired on them?" I asked.

"No. No one has that power. It's not possible to take away someone's powers," Carlisle said.

"A siphon can." Kol met my eyes, speaking for the first time in a while. He studied my reaction.

"What's a siphon?" I asked.

"Those don't exist," Tristan interrupted.

"I've heard my parents speak of a tale—I can't recall the entire story. I was just interested in what a siphon was, so I glazed over the details." He then turned to me and said, "A siphon is someone who can take a supernatural's powers."

"Wait. Do you think I'm a siphon? Is that what I do?"

Rahl stood abruptly. "I must check on something. I will interrogate everyone before I leave. You three. We will talk soon. Keep your heads low and protect Vi," he told his heirs firmly, then came to me and dropped a kiss on my head. Mr. Wilson followed behind him.

There was an awkward silence around the room. The princes glared at Kol and Carlisle, while the two ignored them. "Do you think Vi is a siphon?" Carlisle asked Kol.

He frowned and thought for a minute. "It's possible. At least with what happened with those two Casters."

"What about the fight in combat class? No one lost their powers then," Sebastian asked.

"No. If we're going to consider siphon, then we need to consider mimic." Carlisle wore his thinking face. He often had this expression when had me doing a series of exercises. "It fits the events of the combat class and in Mr. Wilson's office."

"How can she have two rare powers?" Kol asked. Again, his expression was unreadable.

Carlisle shrugged. "It's the only thing that fits so far. I'll do more research. Kol, do you think you can find out more from your parents?"

"Yes. I can." Kol's green eyes met mine.

"Thanks for your help. Both of you." I smiled, feeling extra grateful that these two gorgeous and powerful boys were helping me.

"Why are you two so invested in Vi?" Tristan narrowed his eyes as he studied them closely. His possessiveness was resurfacing.

"Mr. Wilson asked us to be," Carlisle said casually, but then he glanced at me and gave me a look I couldn't determine.

"Why are you involved, bloodsucker? I thought you changed your mind." Sebastian straightened up and crossed his arms. His muscles were bulging through his long-sleeved Henley.

Kol rolled his eyes but then looked at me again. My stomach fluttered every time he directed his intense stare my way. Wait, I couldn't possibly be interested in him as well. I had two mates already. What the fuck? "I have been trying to diffuse the situation with my kin, Vi. Especially Carla. It was why I couldn't risk starting our training sessions, nor could I send word." His eyes begged me to understand.

I nodded, and I noticed a minute change in his tense posture. Was he worried that I was mad at him? That thought gave me tingles down my spine. I locked in my thoughts to make sure my mates wouldn't catch that I was lusting over the Vampire prince. I was a greedy bitch. Apparently, two hot mates weren't enough; I was crushing on the prince. I knew there was no chance for us to be together since I heard Shay and Lori talk about his betrothal to Carla. The thought made me want to punch something.

"Although, it looks like our training is unnecessary since you haven't attacked anyone lately." His lips lifted, which made his handsome face even more out of this world. Kol was beautiful even with his serious face, but when he smiled, it was breathtaking. I had to pry my eyes away from his face as I guiltily glanced at my mates, who missed nothing. They wore identical scowls and were staring daggers at Kol.

"Will you four focus for one second?" Carlisle snapped.

Heat flooded my face since I didn't even realize I was being obvious. Please kill me now.

"We need a plan. The coven will be here and will be very interested in Vi. We can't let them get their hands on her." He looked at each of us to stress the severity of the situation. We all heeded his warning, my boy problem overpowered by fear.

"What would they want with me?" I whispered.

"The coven is full of power-hungry witches." Kol's eyes darkened.

"They weren't always this way. It was peaceful when Carlisle's family was in charge. Now, the Casters desire to rise in power and control all supernaturals, which has the royals warring against each other," Sebastian said. His hand settled on my shoulder, giving me some comfort, while Tristan kept hold of my hand.

"How did they take over from your family?"

Carlisle's jaw tensed, and anger filled his eyes. "The current leader defeated my grandmother. It's how supernaturals chose their leader. The role is passed down through generations, or it's earned by death." He opened his mouth to say more but didn't continue.

I watched him, waiting to see if he would share more.

"Rumors have it that the previous coven leader was betrayed by someone close to her. That was the only way to defeat the high priestess. They become too powerful since they draw powers from their people, so it's almost unheard of for someone to defeat them," Kol said.

I turned to Carlisle, hoping he would confirm Kol's statement. The power in him surged along with his anger. "Our aunt is an ambitious woman. Usually, covens stay within the family, but she betrayed ours and joined another. She is now the right hand of the high priestess."

My energy surged to greet his. His energy called to mine. Ours matched— something I had paid little attention to until now. Whenever he used his powers, I would recognize my slumbering Caster abilities. Oddly, I had Shifter and Caster powers. I wonder if I had Vampire powers as well?

"Umm...why are you looking at me like that?" Carlisle asked, the tip of his ears red as he shifted in his seat.

"I'm sorry. I didn't mean to stare. It's just that your powers call to mine." His eyes grew, and he said nothing.

Kol stiffened up next to him. "Are you sure?"

Did I say something wrong? "I think so? I didn't realize what it was before, but mine surface and I can feel it in my skin whenever I feel his energy. Like he's calling to mine."

"Impossible," Carlisle said mostly to himself, his tone one of disbelief.

"What's going on? Why don't you two share to the room what you're geeking out about," Tristan drawled.

"Casters don't have mates, but they have what you call energy partners. Their powers are compatible, yin and yang, which results in a symbiotic and stable power. It's something most Casters try to achieve," Kol said with bitter undertones.

"Aren't you a wealth of knowledge," Sebastian said as he and Tristan looked at the other two like they were dirt on their shoes.

What was going on with these guys? There must be history between them, something I didn't want to get involved in.

"I need to look more into it. We need to know if this has something to do with your siphon powers," he said and got up without looking me in the eye. I mean, I couldn't blame him. I probably would freak out as well if I found I had over two mates. The heirs made sense. They were so close and were always together as a package deal, and there was a shortage of alpha males. If I added more mates, then what would that make me? However, I couldn't deny that there was something about Kol and not particularly about Carlisle but his powers and mine definitely had an undeniable connection.

"I don't think it needs to be said but lie low. We can't let the Casters get a hold of Vi. Not only for her sake but for the sake of the supernatural community." Carlisle held my eyes and then left.

Soon, Kol followed without a word to any of us.

Fear gripped me, and I couldn't bear being alone that night. We ended up sleeping in Tristan's bed. It was a tight squeeze, but we didn't mind since the two of them liked to snuggle, which had me sleeping soundly throughout the night.

Chapter 9

The princes and I had a long discussion in the living room, which made us miss breakfast.

"You heard Kol, and as much as I hate to admit it, I agree with the bloodsucker. You need to lie low, which means no attending classes," Sebastian said.

"We need to act normal, or else we look guilty," Tristan argued.

Without a firm opinion on the matter, I kept quiet. I didn't really know what the coven was capable of. From what I'd heard so far, they sounded horrible. I trusted my mates to keep me safe. However, I was really looking forward to speaking with Rahl. He should be able to give us better advice and understanding on what to expect. "Perhaps we should speak with Mr. Williams?"

"I'll speak with him while you two stay put. Don't go anywhere until you hear from me," Sebastian said over his shoulder.

My phone dinged, and I opened the group message trail I had going with Shay and Lori. I told them about what happened and why I didn't make it to breakfast.

We'll be on the lookout, Shay texted.

Stay safe, Lori followed.

Love you, guys, I responded. Grateful to have two fierce and loyal best friends.

"Have you heard from Rahl?" I turned to Tristan, who had been studying me since Sebastian left.

"No. He'll reach out when he's ready," Tristan said distractedly.

"What is it?" I raised a brow in question. "Why are you looking at me like that?"

He shook his head. "I'm trying to study your wolf signature. It definitely feels different from other Shifters, so it could explain the siphon theory. Still, it doesn't explain the mate bond. We can only bond with true alphas, so you have to be a wolf Shifter."

The uneasiness in me lessened with his words. I had buried it in the back of my mind because I didn't want to lose what I had with the princes, but the nagging fear of my true mates being taken from me had been eating away at me. "So, do you think we're true mates?" My heart stuttered as the words escaped me.

"Yes. No question about that. A mating bond is a sacred bond, one formed by higher powers. It can't be tampered with," Tristan said with no hesitation.

My heart restarted, and without thought, I went to him, needing to feel his touch. I pressed my mouth firmly to his lips. "I'm glad you said that," I whispered; my voice still raw with emotions.

"Never think otherwise. I'll burn the world down if you're taken from me, Vi." His eyes blazed in anger briefly, then he kissed my temple as he gripped me.

We stayed in the peaceful silence for a few moments until Sebastian walked in the room. He came straight to me and pulled me to my feet. "I heard what you two were just talking about, and I share Tristan's sentiment. No one will take you away from us. If they do, we will raise hell to get you back." He pulled me close and kissed me, which was filled with promise, and left me without a doubt in his words. "We need to go."

"What's going on?"

"Where are we going?" Tristan stood and studied Sebastian.

"We need to go to Mr. Wilson's office. We're definitely not going to class. He'll tell you more but stay vigilant."

His words kept us on alert as we quickly made our way to the dean's office. As we were passing the quad, Kol suddenly appeared next to us. The princes halted, flanking me, and posed for an attack. "Jesus, Kol, you scared me."

"We must hurry," he said with an urgent tone after a brief glance at me.

He made the alarming situation even tenser. I clung to the princes, my fingers digging into their skin. My eyes darted around my surroundings as we briskly walked through the quad. There wasn't anything unusual, except the yard was almost empty. Usually, students would be leisurely walking or congregating.

"Let's keep going. We'll talk more when we're safely inside," Kol hissed over his shoulder.

The knots in my stomach eased as we made it to Mr. Wilson's office. The thud of the door as it shut completely soothed the tension inside of me. The fear was replaced with irritation as I noticed Rahl in the room, sitting next to Carlisle and Mr. Wilson. "Can someone please tell me what's going on before I start freaking out?" I glared at them one at a time, but my eyes settled on Rahl. Why didn't he call for us?

Instead of answering, Rahl got up and gave me a hug. "I know that look, Vi. I just got here, and I'm sorry I had to run out so quickly. I needed to make sure before we proceed."

My anger dissipated. I missed him, and he was my only family left. As my father figure, I couldn't stay mad at him for long. I nodded as I hugged him back. Now that Rahl was here, I felt assured that he had a plan.

"What's going on?" Tristan asked, tugging on my hand then leading me to sit next to Sebastian on the long couch. They each took hold of my hands.

"It's as I feared," Mr. Wilson said in a grave voice. "There is a division in school. Shifters against Vampires and Casters."

The princes stiffened up next to me and looked pointedly at Kol and Carlisle.

"You know where I stand. A few of my people don't want to get involved. It's mostly Logan and Carla's crew," Kol said in a dark tone. His gaze darted to our clasped hands.

"So, you're saying you lost control over your people? Some prince you are," Tristan said.

Kol stood abruptly, cold radiating from him. His eyes turned red.

Tristan and Sebastian shifted their weight to get up and meet his challenge, but I held on to their hands tightly and said, "Kol, I appreciate everything you have done for me. I can't thank you enough for being here and the support you've shown." He directed his red gaze towards me, and I wasn't triggered by it. He didn't remind me of the monster in the alley. Instead, I wanted to wrap my arms around him. We held each other's gaze until his gorgeous greens returned. Even then, he didn't look away right away.

"Vi is right. We need to stand together, and we need all the help we can get." Rahl must have been oblivious of the moment I shared with Kol as he kept glaring at the princes.

"Yes, the Casters won't openly defy the high priestess, but there's a good number that are neutral and would like to reserve judgment on Vi," Carlisle said without looking at me. In fact, he hadn't met my eyes since I got inside the room. I looked at him, expecting him to look at me, but nothing.

Okay, he was acting weird.

"Do your kin know you're here? Are you blowing your cover?" I asked Kol.

"It doesn't matter now. I think it's time to take a stand and set an example." Kol shrugged. Even though his body language and tone of voice was nonchalant, his eyes were hard, and there was a hint of tension in his jaw. I knew he was feeling more than what he was letting on.

"Will this cause an issue with Carla's family?" Mr. Wilson asked.

His eyes darted to me quickly before he answered. "Perhaps. But as the princes callously pointed out, I need to make a firm stand. Then I will see who's in my corner." He crossed his leg over his knee and leaned back with his chin high, looking like a true, noble prince.

"What a mess. All this just because of me?" I whispered. "What if I left and went home with you? I didn't even want to be here in the first place," I asked Rahl.

There was a chorus of disagreement from the princes, Kol, and Carlisle. My brow raised in surprise as I stared at Kol and Carlisle. I slowly turned to Rahl, who said, "I would like to keep that as a last resort. This will mean war. We've been toeing the line for years, but this time, as Kol said, it might be time to make a stand."

"I can't possibly cause war. I don't even understand what's going on. It makes little sense," I insisted as I got up forcefully in frustration and paced behind the couch.

"Vi, listen to me." Rahl stood close to me, his tone demanding. I turned to him, then crossed my arms. "The royals have been on the verge of war for years, ever since the high priestess took over. Her quest to dominate the supernaturals had been obvious from the beginning. She's just great at covering her tracks so we've never been able to come up with something concrete to put on her. However, I wouldn't be surprised if they didn't know that the school currently houses a siphon—and a mimic to boot." He paused with a shake of his head. He looked at me firmly and said, "They will stop at nothing to own you now that they have a rallying cry since two of their own were injured. They will insist that we hand you over. If we refuse, they will wage war."

I cocked my head with a frown. "What did you call me?" I looked around, and everyone had a curious and almost fearful look on their faces.

"It's what I had to check on yesterday. Kol's tale sparked something in my memory, and I had to confirm what I knew about the forbidden powers." He sat back down and continued. "Siphons and mimics used to walk amongst the supernaturals. However, they were hunted down for their unique powers until they became extinct. It took many generations since a single one could take out an entire army of supernaturals. We don't know their exact origin. We just know that they are powerful. They keep to themselves, so there isn't much information about them. The only recorded information we have are accounts of their abilities as we witnessed them." He looked to Mr. Wilson, whose gaze was locked on me.

Rahl turned to me with troubled eyes. "Siphons can absorb powers and drain a supernatural dry. They can take the power and use it for their own. Meanwhile, mimics can do the same thing, but they cannot take away power. They are just as powerful as siphons because they can absorb a limitless amount of skill, and it never wanes. We are uncertain if the siphons run out of power or if they, like mimics, can keep the power forever."

I stared at him, speechless, then I gazed at the princes who looked just as lost as I was. "And you think I'm a siphon or a mimic? I mean, how is that even possible?" I looked to the others, hoping they would aid me and tell Rahl his theory was insane.

"I don't know, Vi. From my research, you definitely have mimic and siphon powers, but I'm also certain you're a Shifter." He shrugged, then turned to Mr. Wilson in question.

"Yes. I sense Shifter energy from her, along with Vampire and Caster. Which is not possible, so that could be the siphon or mimic I'm feeling, but the Shifter is certain."

I leaned back, somewhat appeased. At least that was confirmed. "If I have siphon and mimic powers, then they're not really extinct, are they? I mean, since I'm here."

"Actually, we've never heard of someone being both a Shifter and a mimic. There are only records of one or the other, but never both," Mr. Wilson said.

"I agree. I used my grandmother's private library, and the information only accounted for one or the other," Carlisle said, meeting my eyes for the first time. His eyes softened, and he said, "We need to do further testing to see if our energies are truly compatible, but it isn't important at this time. We'll find the time when everything settles." His eyes shifted to the side once again, avoiding mine.

Why is he acting so weird about this? I eyed him for a minute, trying to decipher how he felt about the possibility of our energies being compatible, but he showed no emotions. I felt for Tristan and Sebastian's feelings, but they had their shields up. He was right; this was best addressed when the coven wasn't after me.

"It would definitely be easier if we knew your parents, but since we have no clue where to even begin, we just need to address the most pressing issue." Rahl looked around the room. My chest tightened in fear as I watched his tense shoulders and severe expression. "We need to make sure the Casters don't get their hands on Vi. They will stop at nothing to get their hands on her." He looked at each one of the boys. "I can't stress this enough: Vi's powers in the wrong hands could cause irreparable damage to the supernatural community."

I couldn't help but glance at Mr. Williams and wondered if his allegiance fell to the current priestess. Carlisle was understandable, but I wasn't sure about the dean. He must have seen my glance because he said, "You must wonder if I agree with the current coven leadership?" He raised his eyebrows, then continued before I answered. "I don't. The Parkers are close family friends of mine, and Margaret was my mentor. Her death was a significant loss to the Casters and for me personally. Furthermore, I disagree with the current priestess' policies and her approach to other supernaturals."

Shame filled me for doubting the dean, and I didn't know what to say to make it right, so I just nodded.

"What do you recommend we do?" Tristan asked.

"When do you expect a visit from the coven?" Sebastian followed.

"It'll be any day now," Carlisle said.

"I recommend you try to stick together and continue your routine. It's important to show a united front. Unfortunately, the time for subtleties is over. It's time to take a stand." Rahl spoke mostly to Kol, who nodded his confirmation to the king of Shifters. They exchanged unspoken words with the look they shared, which made me feel better. At least we had the Vampire prince on our side.

Determination filled the air, and a feeling of security flooded me. Knowing that my mates, Kol, and Carlisle, would be by my side allowed me some semblance of courage as I faced the unknown threat the coven brought.

My head jerked to Rahl as he said, "I will speak with you three soon. I'll see you in your room after I finish up with a few things here."

My eyes grew wide from the sudden dismissal, and I looked to Tristan, whose eyes narrowed. Why was he dismissing us so suddenly?

Sebastian, however, stood and reached for my hand and gestured for us to follow. I caught Kol's and Carlisle's eyes and smiled at them on my way out. One of these days, I would find a way to thank them properly for their support.

As we walked through the quad, I wasn't as scared as I was on the way to the dean's office. Shay and Lori ran towards us as we were halfway through the enormous expanse of the open quad. Their enthusiasm almost brought me to the ground as they both tackled me and clutched me in a tight embrace.

"Oh my god, I thought something had happened to you," Shay said.

"Where have you been?" Lori asked.

"It's a long story. I'm sorry I scared you."

"We need to get back to the room." Sebastian glanced nervously at a group of Vampires up ahead.

"So, you've heard then?" Shay asked as she and Lori hooked their arms through mine.

"It's been super crazy. There's a fight in every classroom. Each supernatural for themself," Lori said in a sad tone.

"This is crazy," I whispered.

Tristan walked ahead of us while Sebastian flanked our back. We avoided the group and gave them a wide berth, but they deliberately stood in our way...

"Look what we have here, guys. The Vampire hater," a tall boy with black hair and black eyes said over Tristan's shoulder. Three other boys and two girls surrounded him. They all flashed their fangs at us, and their eyes were tinged with red. Anger and fear surged inside me, but I didn't want to make a move in fear of injuring my mates and my friends. We were outnumbered, and I would never forgive myself if something were to happen to them.

"We don't have beef with you, so back off and let us pass," Tristan growled with his shoulders taut and his fists tight. Shay and Lori held on to my arms. I wanted to push them behind me, but I didn't want to start anything. I even held my breath and made myself small.

Soon, a group of Shifters stood to our left to support our group. However, Casters joined the Vampires.

Guys, this is getting out of hand. We don't need a brawl in the middle of the quad, I warned.

Tristan partially shifted as the six Vampires' eyes were now completely red.

The air filled with tension as each group sized each other up, waiting for the other to make a move. The pressure reached a breaking point, and I was sure I was minutes from throwing up in fear.

"Enough!" someone called in a booming and commanding voice that had the Vampires dropping on one knee. "I've had enough of your insubordination! You will not threaten my father's legacy and tarnish our name. Anyone caught starting a fight against another supernatural will answer directly to me." Kol glared at the Vampires and then turned to us. "I will sort this out and be assured that I will not be merciful." Kol's authoritative presence as he stood over the Vampires had the quad in silence. His expression was cold and unmerciful. The Vampires didn't move a muscle. They kept their heads bowed as Kol turned to the rest of us and declared in a forceful tone that left no doubt, "The Vampires will not take part in this strife. We remain at peace with all supernaturals." His icy gaze landed on the Casters, and he continued to walk without looking at me or anyone else as his Vampires parted for him. They followed behind him with their heads bowed.

That impressive display of authority had left me breathless—hot damn. If I wasn't about to pee my pants from fear, I would drool over Kol right now. But my eyes darted to the Casters, who still stood awkwardly in front of us. Albeit they looked more uneasy as the crowd thinned significantly.

Tristan hadn't moved a muscle, his feral focus directed towards the Casters. But they didn't engage. Instead, they thinned out without another word. A sigh of relief escaped me as Sebastian nudged for me to walk. I felt his sharp claws on my back, which meant he was still partially shifted.

No one said a word until we reached the safety of the room.

"Why didn't the Casters engage us?" I sagged on the couch with my knees still slightly trembling.

"They didn't have the numbers. Without the Vampires, they didn't have the upper hand," Sebastian said.

"No offense, but I'm really curious. How can other supernaturals stand against Casters? I mean, they have magic. They can practically do anything."

Shay snorted.

Lori rolled her eyes at Shay and turned to me with a patient look. "Every supernatural has a weakness. While Vampires and Shifters have strength, speed, and quick healing, Casters possess a human weakness. Their energies and skills are also limited, meaning they need to make their spells count. Besides, Vampires are difficult to kill, and Shifter's hides resist most magical spells. So, it's an even playing field."

"So, what do we do now?" I asked and wrapped my arms around myself. "I can't believe this is happening because of me."

Shay draped her arm around me as she sat next to me, followed by Lori. "Girl, this is not all because of you. You might be the catalyst, but this is a long time coming."

"Yes. The Casters have been itching to move against the rest of us, but they lacked support. Now they are using you. I'm sure the head of the coven will take advantage of this situation and push her selfish agenda," Lori said with a frown.

"It's still my fault. I shouldn't have come to this school. Maybe I should leave. If they can't find me, then they have nothing."

"Remember what Uncle said. We need to stay put. That will be our last resort." Tristan stood behind the couch with his arms crossed. He was still filled with tension, which I felt through our bond.

Before I could argue, Sebastian voiced what had been nagging at me. I could disappear and hide in the human world. It would be like the last few months never happened.

"If you go, we go, and we can't abandon our people, Vi," Sebastian said in a grave tone.

Well, when he put it like that, I really had no choice. Plus, I really didn't want to leave my mates. I also knew that they would find me wherever I went. Our bond would make sure of that. That left me trapped and used as a pawn in a war among the supernaturals.

"What do you recommend we do then?" I snapped. *I didn't mean to take my frustration out on them. Why was this happening to me? I just wanted to be left alone. I didn't want to fight for my life and hurt someone or watch someone get hurt. Why me?*

I don't know why you, baby, but you're special. I've known it from the moment I laid eyes on you, Sebastian said through our bond. My head snapped in his direction. I wasn't aware that I shared my thoughts with them.

Don't worry. You're not alone. No matter what, we will always be by your side, Tristan said firmly.

Warmth spread inside of me, and my nerves settled, but guilt reared its ugly head. *I'm sorry I snapped at you before.*

Sebastian pulled my hips to his and encircled me with his warm embrace. I let out a deep breath and melted into his arms, allowing myself the comfort of his touch for just a moment before facing the problem.

We waited for Rahl while Lori and Shay said their goodbyes. They promised to go straight to their room and to meet up with us first thing tomorrow. Most likely, they would be targets as well because of their association with me.

We sat in tense silence for over an hour until finally Rahl walked in, not bothering to knock.

"Okay. I have little time. I need to get my guys ready. However, I wanted to speak with the three of you." He towered over us, not bothering to sit as we looked up at him from the couch. He studied all three of us and lingered on Sebastian's hand on my leg and Tristan's arm over my shoulder. "I noticed that you three formed a bond." He paused, watching our reaction.

I glanced worriedly at the princes, worried that they would get in trouble, but they both had big, proud smiles. "It just happened," I said as an explanation.

"Don't get me wrong, Vi." His lips turned up on one side. "I'm really proud of my heirs. I'm floored. Usually, we would throw a big celebration and present you to everyone." He looked away with sadness and disappointment in his eyes. "But these are troubled times. So, we can't partake in any of our usual celebrations. Although, I wanted to personally say that I'm very pleased with the turn of events." He stretched out his hand, and I took it and stood in front of him. He placed his other hand on top of the one he already held and gazed down at me. His eyes twinkled, and he said, "I already think of you as one of my own, but I am glad that you are now officially family. As the mate to my heirs, you will be the queen of Shifters one day, and I couldn't be more pleased. As our future queen and family, we protect our own. We won't let the coven touch you," he said firmly.

I blinked back tears at his words. My throat tightened, and I wrapped my arms around him. "Thank you, Rahl. You're my only family left," I whispered. His arms tightened around me, and we held each other for a moment. He then looked at my mates. "You watch over her. I'll do my part. If things get bad, you know where to go."

Tristan nodded and pulled me in his arms, then clutched my hip close.

Sebastian took hold of my hand. "We'll make sure nothing happens to her. You have our word, Uncle."

He turned back to me. "Train hard with the guys and learn to protect yourself. You can't rely on others to always be there." Then Rahl stepped close and kissed the top of my head. "You three stick together and watch out for each other." He gave us all a pointed look and patted the princes' shoulders on his way out.

Confidence filled me. We would emerge from this fine because I got a lot of support from my mates, Rahl, Kol, Carlisle, and Mr. Wilson.

Chapter 10

I stayed up late into the night in Tristan's bed with Sebastian on one side and Tristan on the other as we discussed a plan and a training schedule. We finally decided to stay the course and attended class as usual. We needed to show everyone that we weren't afraid. The Shifter community had to stick together and show no fear—their leaders couldn't afford to show weakness.

It was weird thinking of myself as a leader. I was still wrapping my head around the thought that I would one day be their queen. It was too much to process, so I tried not to think about it. For now, I was just enjoying the time I had with my mates.

That night, I dreamt of my mom and woke up feeling relaxed and less fearful. Sleeping in the arms of my mates gave me a night of restful sleep, I've only had a few since my mom passed. It was also my first dream of her without waking up crying.

Rubbing her necklace that was tucked under my shirt gave me the courage and determination I needed. My mom's memory gave me strength and served as a reminder to not allow others to take advantage of those less powerful. I hated power-hungry bullies, like Logan. These coven witches were no different.

I would no longer cower and be helpless as I watched my loved ones get hurt. If I were truly powerful, they would feel my wrath. If they refused to leave me be then, they would regret that choice.

Sebastian rubbed his thumb on my forehead, followed by a light kiss. "What got into your head?"

My mouth curved into a smile. "Nothing. Who would have thought you were sweet?" I countered.

"I'm still me. You just bring out a certain side of me." His mouth lingered close to my mouth, teasing me. Memories of our time together flashed in my mind. He must have thought the same thing because his molten eyes captured mine, and for a moment, I was sure we both thought of going back inside the room.

"No time for that, you two. We'll be late for class." Tristan emerged from the room and kissed my cheek. He gathered our things and handed me my backpack. His lips quirked up, and he said, "Although, I would like to revisit that thought tonight when we all get back to the room." He winked and walked out. Wait, did he mean the three of us together? At the same time? I gaped at his back, and I looked at Sebastian, who had an amused look on his face, and followed Tristan. My face flushed at the thought, but the idea lingered and had me impatient to be done with the day.

"Hey, Vi. Earth to Vi." Shay waved a hand in front of my face.

"Sorry. I was preoccupied." My ears burned from embarrassment while Shay gave me an understanding look, then glared around the room. She must have thought I was worried about the students. I kept my mouth shut and tried to pay attention to what she was saying. I peeked at Tristan, who wore a ghost of a smile, then at Sebastian, who met my gaze with the same heat as earlier. The tip of my ears heated, and I turned to Shay and Lori.

"Our pack said the same thing," Lori said.

I bowed my head and picked at my usual breakfast to hide that I wasn't following their conversation.

"Yes, we were instructed to stick together and not to go anywhere alone. Everyone is taking this seriously, and they are ready. They're sick of pretending to not know what the Casters are after," Shay said in between bites of something with red sauce. After a drink of her juice, she continued, "Don't worry, Vi. No one blames you."

I looked around the cafeteria, which looked emptier than usual. There weren't as many Vampires around. I wondered if Kol had something to do with that. Although, I got the same stares and nasty looks from others. I noticed the Shifters smiled or wave at me. Some even said hi. However, some Vampires purposely avoid my gaze.

"Yes. The Shifters are behind you a hundred percent!" Lori said, not looking up from her large plate of hash browns.

I flashed them a grateful smile. "Thanks, guys. That really means a lot to me." It also brought me peace to know that my friends would be safe. I'd seen their pack mates. They were tough.

"Let's go, ladies. We don't want to be late." Tristan stood behind me. His voice was light, and his expression relaxed, but his eyes darted around the room now and then. Sebastian just scowled at everyone. It was like he was back to his old, grumpy self. However, when our eyes met, his gaze warmed, and I would feel his emotions through our bond.

Admittedly, my bond with my mates had developed at lightning speed, but it felt natural. They came at a time I needed them the most. Even though I'd coped with the loss of my mom, I'd still felt alone. Sometimes, I'd had thoughts that no one would miss me if I were to follow her. Or when times were tough, I'd often questioned what the point in trying was. Every day it had gotten tougher to listen to the small voice inside me that told me to continue to fight since I couldn't find the reason for living. If it weren't for Rahl, I would have given up. He gave me a purpose and a reason to fight. The obsession with trying to find my past got me through. Although, I knew in the back of my mind that it wasn't sustainable. I feared that once I didn't have that, I would succumb to the voice inside of me telling me to give up.

Now, I had a fire inside of me that flared hot. I associated that feeling with my mates. They had become my reason for trying. So, regardless of how fast our relationship had progressed or how little time I'd known them, it didn't bother me. I embraced it and was grateful for it.

"You keep disappearing in your head today. Are you sure you're okay?" Tristan whispered in my ear.

"Yes. I'm sorry. I'm just having a sort of revelation." I shrugged.

"Should we be worried?" Sebastian asked.

I clasped his hand to mine and squeezed. *Never,* I said to both of them through our bond.

Everyone glanced at us and acknowledged us as they made their way to their seats. Shay and Lori had their brows raised with how much attention we were getting from the other Shifters.

"We won't linger for long in this room today. Your specialized class has a lot of important topics to go over, so let's all make our way there," Professor Wilkins said.

We all shared a surprised look but made our way to our class. I hugged Shay and Lori. "I'll see you two later. Be careful and stick close together."

"We will," Lori said. Shay turned to the princes and said, "You two take care of our girl, you hear."

Tristan smiled as Sebastian gathered my backpack and clasped my hand.

I waved at the girls and followed the guys to Professor Wilkin's classroom. This time we all sat together. The professor eyed us closely but said nothing. However, I didn't miss the twinkle in his eyes.

"We wanted to speak with each of you to prepare for the upcoming war. The king instructed us to make this a priority, so here we are. We are going to take this time to make sure we prepare you to defend yourselves...just in case."

My heart sped up in nervousness, but I didn't feel the crippling fear I did yesterday. Today I was determined, so I listened to every word the professor said. "I believe we practiced partial shifting last time. We will go over this once more, and then each of you will shift." Tristan snorted, which the professor didn't miss. With an eyebrow raised, he asked, "Mr. Cormel, do you have anything to say?"

"No, sir," Tristan answered.

Mr. Wilkin trained his eyes on Tristan for a few more moments, then turned to Sebastian. "Can you tell Mr. Cormel why it's important to learn how to shift quickly?"

Sebastian looked like he wanted to smile, but he answered, "During a shift is when a shifter is most vulnerable. The precious seconds it takes to shift could mean your life when you're in a battle."

Sure, golden boy. You're such a kiss-ass, Tristan said.

This kiss-ass can probably beat your time in shifting, Sebastian countered.

Oh, you're on, Tristan said.

I wanted to tell the two of them to shield and keep it to themselves because I really wanted to hear what the professor was saying. But they were freaking amusing.

"...after you partially shift, you can shift completely, then shift back. I will time you. Who wants to go first?"

"I do," both Tristan and Sebastian said at the same time.

I chuckled, and Mr. Wilkins eyed them suspiciously. "Sebastian, go ahead."

Sebastian stood at the front and faced Tristan and me. His fingers elongated into claws, and then his eyes flashed yellow. Next stood his wolf before us. I had to blink because he shifted so fast it was almost instantaneous.

Tristan tutted next to me. "Show off," he muttered as Sebastian sat back in his chair. When Tristan stood, his claws were already extended, and the wolf was looking out from behind his eyes. As he took a step, he transformed into a wolf. How were they doing it so fast?

"Okay, boys, that was impressive. Clearly, you don't need practice. Vi?"

"Professor, what were our times?" Tristan asked.

The professor looked at him in confusion, then looked down at his paper. "It was hard to time since it happened almost instantaneously. You both did great!"

Tristan smirked at Sebastian, who rolled his eyes.

"Vi?"

It was my turn to step forward. I had no trouble with my partial shift. However, it took me a while to shift to a full wolf.

"Shift back, Ms. Price, and then go again," Mr. Wilkins said.

Easier said than done. I sniffed the air, and my snout turned in my mate's direction. My tail wagged. I wanted to play with my mates. I felt their wolves respond through our bond.

Focus, Vi, Sebastian said.

I calmed my mind, ignored the distracting sounds and smells of my surroundings, and thought of my clothes and the human form. Eventually, I transformed back.

"Let's do that a few more times. I don't expect you to be at the princes' level, but it needs to be faster than that. In the meantime, I want you both to read up on how to protect yourselves against hexes and curses. Also, read the section on counter curses while I work with Ms. Price."

I shifted back and forth possibly several dozen times before the bell rang. I was definitely more fluid and quicker in my shift by the end of the class. "Well done, everyone. Remember to not start anything and to be alert," the professor called to our backs.

The princes walked me to my next class. I turned to say goodbye as we reached the front of the class, but Tristan walked in. I grasped Sebastian's arm to stop him. "What are you two doing? You don't take this class."

"I thought we were clear this morning. We're not leaving your side," Sebastian said as he walked in after Tristan.

"But what about your classes?" I asked as I caught up with him. We were getting stares from the kids in the room, but I ignored them. I followed the guys and sat at the back where Tristan was. "We have it all sorted out. Don't worry, Vi," Sebastian reassured me.

Professor Taylor walked in and said nothing about the princes sitting in his class, so I relaxed. I ignored the other students' looks, just like I did in the cafeteria and the hallway.

"Today, I wanted to discuss the reign of Hakuba. She was the mystic coven leader. She was vicious and hunted down any other magic wielder that wasn't considered a Caster. Although there are only three major supernaturals recognized, we suspect there are others, like the Fae, who are not in this world. However, we have stories of encounters with them. There are plenty of other species, which we call unknowns, that her coven hunted down. Anyone that showed signs of magic, they took down." He looked through the windows with worried eyes, then turned to us. His eyes locked on mine and he continued.

"The other two rulers worried that her goal was to start another war. She was power-hungry, after all. So, the other sups gathered allies, including some from the Caster community, to take Hakuba down from within. They convinced a young Margaret Parker, who had no desire to rule but was whispered to be more powerful than the sitting priestess. It took close to a year to convince her. It wasn't until her cousin died protecting someone that Hakuba wanted to eliminate. Priestess Margaret defeated Hakuba to avenge her beloved cousin and ruled for several centuries. Her nephew, Carlisle Parker, was supposed to take over. However, when she fell ill, the current priestess and Margaret's former second-in-command took advantage of her weakness and defeated her. It was rumored that even in her weakened state, she dealt a crippling blow to the two." His lips quirked on the side, and his eyes shone in glee, like he enjoyed the knowledge that they hurt the current coven leader.

Oh my god. Did he mean Carlisle? My magic mentor was the true wizard heir? This knowledge floored me.

"Priestess Margaret was an outstanding leader. Her reign was filled with peace and growth within the Casters. Her coven worked well with the other two rulers, which allowed the supernatural community to grow and prosper regardless of the restrictions the human government sanctioned on us. With the current..."

We all turned as we heard a knock on the door. A tall male student walked in and whispered something to Mr. Taylor, who frowned and said something in response. The student shook his head, then they both looked in my direction.

I stiffened up, and I felt the two princes tense next to me.

Mr. Taylor had a troubled look as he met my eyes. "Ms. Price, you are being summoned."

He looked like he wanted to convey something, but he couldn't. I nodded and gathered my things. Tristan grabbed my backpack and stood along with Sebastian.

"They only called for Violet. No one else. I was told to only bring her." The boy frowned.

"If Vi goes, we go. Otherwise, you can go back and tell your superior she's not going anywhere," Tristan snapped.

The kids in class quietly watched the exchange. The boy turned to Professor Taylor, hoping he would intervene, but the professor shrugged. "I can't defy the king's orders. You and your coven can take it up with the king," he said.

So, it's the coven. What do we do? I asked the guys.

Nothing. Let's see what they want. No one makes a move unless they do, Sebastian said. He grabbed my hand, and we followed the boy out. Professor Taylor gave me a small nod, which I appreciated. It seemed like he was on my side.

"Where are we meeting the coven?" I asked. I felt Tristan's irritation and anger towards the boy. I squeezed his hand, and he took a deep breath out.

"In the dean's office," he said.

At least we'd have the dean for support.

I'm texting Uncle, Sebastian said as he lagged behind us. I felt better knowing that Rahl was aware of the coven's presence. Although, I was sure he was already informed.

The boy knocked and entered before someone answered. We walked in, and instead of Mr. Wilson sitting behind the desk, it was a skinny woman with a long, pointy nose. Her dark hair had a long grey streak in the front and was pulled into a tight bun. Standing next to her was a short, stout woman with light brown hair and blue eyes, wearing a malicious grin on her face. I shivered as I stepped closer. Their energy felt weird—it felt slimy and sinister. Mr. Wilson sat on one of the chairs in front of the desk.

"Robin, I thought I specifically instructed you to only bring the girl?"

I opened my mouth to say I was standing right in front of her when Sebastian squeezed my hand in warning. That's right, play nice until they make a move. I took a deep breath, trying to control the sudden heat inside of me. This woman triggered the same rage as the bully Vampires in combat class. I clutched at the princes' hands tightly as I controlled my anger.

"I'm sorry, Priestess, but they insisted. Order of the king." He bowed his head, and I felt his fear in the air.

I glared at the woman in front of me, then at Mr. Wilson, who wore a blank expression. Why was she allowed to treat people as such?

Love, calm down. Now is not the time to lose it, Sebastian said.

I took more calming breaths in and noticed the short woman next to her studying me. I met her eyes in defiance, and she flashed me a knowing smile. What was that all about?

"Very well. You are dismissed," the priestess said, and for the first time, she directed her attention to me.

"So, you're the girl who attacked two of my people?"

I opened my mouth to defend myself when Tristan squeezed my hand.

"High Priestess, although I respect your position and I have no quarrel with you, I would appreciate it if you didn't accuse my mate and the future queen of Shifters with such blatant lies," he said in an icy tone.

The woman's eyes grew a fraction wider. Then her head snapped to the stubby lady, then to Mr. Wilson, who shook his head, then to us. "Mate? When did this happen?" she said, clearly surprised.

"We don't divulge such information to others," Sebastian answered.

She stared at the desk for a moment, ignoring Sebastian, and then her gaze flicked towards me. "Nonetheless, she needs to answer for her crimes. Therefore, she must come with us," she said with a jut of her chin.

"Again, as my brother pointed out, you are accusing our mate. Isn't there a process for such instances? Why didn't you bring this up with the king? If you wanted a trial, then isn't that the proper way to do this? Since when does the high priestess deal with mundane crimes like attacks amongst students?"

She opened her mouth to say something, then shut it. Her eyes were burning in anger as she clenched her fists. My eyes flickered to her hands that looked deformed and filled with scars. Is this what Mr. Taylor meant when he said Carlisle's grandmother dealt a crippling blow to the both of them? She noticed what I was staring at and hastily drew her sleeve down to cover her hands.

"You are only an heir and not quite a king yet. My personal affairs are no concern of yours," she snapped.

"When it comes to our mate, then it is definitely our concern," Tristan said coolly.

"She's not going anywhere with you," Sebastian said defiantly.

The high priestess shot up from the chair, her dark energy swirling around her. "Are you challenging me, alpha heir?" she asked in a low voice. Her second-in-command was red-faced and pulled energy to her as well. It was weird how I could see their energy clearly. I'd never been able to see it before. Their threatening postures and show of power triggered something in me. A swirling pit of warmth awoke inside of me. It begged to be released and attack these two Casters who threatened my mate.

Mr. Wilson stretched out his hands. "Let's all calm down. No need to do anything harsh. I'm sure we can talk about this civilly."

The short lady waved a hand towards Mr. Wilson, and I reacted. I thrust my hand but didn't know what I did. I saw nothing except the two Casters, who were both red-faced and looked like they would pop an aneurysm with the way they were glaring at me. Even though I didn't know what I'd done, I straightened my shoulders and said, "Do not attack anyone here."

Before they responded, the door burst open, and Carlisle, Kol, and Rahl walked in. "What is the meaning of this?" Rahl's voice boomed.

I let out a breath of relief. Good. He was here. He would take care of things. I looked back at the two Casters. Instead of fear, there was a subtle glint of glee in their expression that I didn't like. It made me wary and I feared for Rahl.

"Why did I know you would be here, King Rahl?" the priestess said as she straightened up from her aggressive stance. "You're so predictable." The short lady chuckled, then glared at Carlisle.

"Nephew. As usual, you disappoint me. Associating yourself with these creatures." She gestured at us.

"Aunt Rose. Still evil, I see," Carlisle greeted casually.

"You bring powerful allies, Rahl, but they're only children. They have no say in this," the priestess said.

"Lucille, stop this madness. You are embarking on a journey that will only lead to a lot of death," King Rahl said.

"The solution is simple. Give me what I want, and we part peacefully." She cocked a brow as she glanced at me.

"You know I can't do that," King Rahl said.

"Then we are at an impasse."

"It's how you proceed that will dictate the future of supernaturals. If this gets out of hand, the government will step in. This time, they won't give us a second chance. Their numbers are vast, and their technology is more sophisticated than it was in the first war."

"Unlike you, Rahl, I do not fear the pesky humans. They are beneath us. We are naturally the better race, and we deserve to rule them."

"You are not taking down the rest of us with your greed, Lucille."

"Ms. Pruitt, you are out of line, and I suggest you leave," Kol said.

She glanced at Kol and laughed. "Oh, little prince. I appreciate the bravado, but you do not speak for your people."

"I am the Vampire prince. My words are binding. The Vampires condemn this greed."

"Are you certain of that, prince? Have you spoken to your parents?" Her eyes shone with amusement.

Kol, on the other hand, looked shocked. Was it possible for his parents to side with this psycho?

Let's hope not, Tristan said through our bond.

I met Carlisle's eyes, and we both shared a look of worry.

"I received no word or intel that the king supports your actions," Rahl said. He glanced at Mr. Wilson, who shook his head minutely.

Perhaps she's bluffing?

She's too cocky to be bluffing, Sebastian said.

"It's over. Stop this foolishness, Rahl. Hand the girl over, and let's prevent any further conflict. We shall leave here in peace."

"Are you challenging the Shifters, Ms. Pruitt?" Rahl asked in a low voice.

"If it must come to that. You will not stand in my way." She waved a hand, and my breath caught in my throat. My eyes grew in fear as I looked at Rahl. No! I couldn't lose another loved one. I couldn't! But I was too late. I saw her energy sail towards Rahl a second faster than mine did. She was fast, even with her injured hand. Along with the princes, my hands stretched to pull Rahl away, but the dark magic never connected.

I looked around and saw Carlisle with his arms outstretched, concentrating on his energy. The vein on his temple throbbed, and I knew he couldn't hold it long. The priestess drew power from the Caster race. He was no match. I touched Carlisle's energy, and mine sparked to life again, and this time I hurled it at the two. But Rose blocked me. She was thrown a couple steps, and she was bent backward. She looked like she was carrying a heavy load and was about to succumb to its weight.

King Rahl shifted along with my mates, and Kol stood next to me. The wolves circled the witches, but the priestess waved her hand and threw something towards the window, which shattered all the office glass. Kol draped his arms around me, protecting me from the flying glass. The wolves were trying to get through the shield the two witches erected. Carlisle and Mr. Wilson were bent over from exhaustion. They had protected Rahl.

Then we heard a loud explosion, and chaos descended in the academy. I could hear screams and a series of explosions on the grounds. Kol pulled me to the ground. "What's going on?"

"It sounds like the witches attacked the academy. I don't have the power to link with my people yet, so I don't know exactly what's happening outside," he said next to me. Then he glanced worriedly at me. "I need to get you out of here."

"No. We can't leave them." Rahl and the princes were still engaging the Casters.

"He's right. You need to go. It's you they want. I'll protect them," Carlisle said next to us.

I studied him for injuries. Aside from looking tired, he looked fine. I wanted to argue that he didn't look like he was in any state to protect anyone, but then Tristan shifted and was in front of me. Carlisle took Tristan's place and stood next to the wolves, but they couldn't get through the barrier. The Casters were throwing what looked like energy balls at the wolves. It was fortunate that they were not affected by magic. Mr. Wilson looked like he was casting to take down the barrier.

"Kol, you need to take her. More of them will be here soon. There are a lot of them on the grounds. They can't get their hands on Vi," Tristan said.

Kol stood and tugged on my hand.

I pulled my hand away, but Kol held on. "No. I can help and protect you guys. I can't leave you to fight this alone. I can't. Please don't make me." Tears started flowing, and I was back again in the alley, feeling helpless as the Vampire attacked my mom.

"We will find you. We are linked. There is nowhere we couldn't locate you." He kissed my forehead. "Don't worry about us. We can handle the Casters," he said cockily and nodded to Kol. Then he was once again in his wolf form. He didn't look back. He jumped in front of the shield and barreled at it.

I struggled to get free of Kol. I wanted to get to my loved ones, but he used his Vampire strength and speed. He carried me as we flashed in a blur. I soon gave up and leaned my head on his neck and cried. This was again because of me. My mother died because of me. I couldn't forgive myself if anyone was hurt because of me. Why did my strength abandon me? I couldn't break through Kol's hold.

Panic built inside of me. Once again, I struggled against Kol's hold, and my breaths came in short bursts. I worked to get a full breath of air, but I couldn't. I saw black. Then I felt a prick on my neck, and my worry subsided until my vision completely turned black.

Chapter 11

I must have passed out because I woke up to a blinding light from the sun shining from the window. I blinked and burrowed deeper into the pillow and closed my eyes. Perhaps it was just a bad dream. I jerked upright and looked around the unfamiliar room. Then I saw Kol sitting on a chair to the right of the bed, watching me.

His green eyes peered into mine and held them captive for a minute. When our eyes met, it was like I could feel him inside of me. Like we were connected. Then he looked away, and the feeling was gone. I must have hit my head.

"Are you okay?" Kol said as he sat on the bed next to me.

"Yeah, just a little disoriented. Where am I?" I looked at the large room with dark wooden furniture and heavy black drapes on the window.

"You're in my home. It's the safest place I could think of."

Disappointment filled me. It wasn't a dream after all. "Have you heard from anyone?"

He shook his head.

"But what about what the priestess woman implied, that your parents are in league with her?"

He absently tucked a stray hair behind my ear, which brought on butterflies in my stomach. "No, I'm certain my father is not in league with that evil woman," he said firmly. "Regardless, this is my private quarters. No one enters or leaves without my knowledge. You're perfectly safe here, Vi." His voice sounded velvety, like a soft caress in my ear. My eyes lingered on his mesmerizing green eyes while his hand was still on my face.

Then, it was as if I woke up from a trance and my head cleared. What the...

"What is going on? What are you doing to me?"

"I'm sorry, Vi. You're just reacting to my bite."

I hurried away from him until I hit the headboard. "What do you mean?" Then I remembered the prick on my neck. I felt for my neck, but the skin felt smooth.

"I'm sorry. I didn't mean to bite you. But it was the only way I could think of in the moment. You were panicking, and you were losing consciousness, and we needed to escape fast."

"So, you bit me?" My voice rose in disbelief.

"Yes, a Vampire's bite has a euphoric effect," he said in his usual calm, matter-of-fact manner, but his eyes shifted briefly like he was hiding something.

"I'm sorry. Please don't be mad. I've never bitten anyone. It was an emergency. I promise not to do it again unless you ask me to."

Why in the world would I ask him to bite me again? The prince was weird. I looked down, and I still wore the same clothes.

"I did nothing to you. I promise. You passed out, and you've been asleep since then," he said with a look I couldn't describe. The prince was trying hard to put on the blank mask he usually wore around others, but he showed different emotions that I couldn't read and that he was struggling to hide.

The funny thing was, I trusted him. He'd saved me last night, and there was a connection I felt towards him—something I couldn't describe.

"We should eat. We don't know when they'll make contact."

I nodded and got out of bed.

"There are clean clothes in the top drawer. The shower is through that door." He pointed to the door to the right of the room and then to the front. He said, "I will be in the other room past the living room, waiting for you." Then he got up and left.

I watched his back for a moment, trying to decide what it was between us that was different. However, I gave up. I didn't know what it was, except a connection. Something I felt in the beginning with him and Carlisle and the princes, but now it was stronger somehow. I shook my head and sighed. Another mystery to solve on another day. I closed my eyes instead and felt for my mates, but nothing. Instead of worrying and having another meltdown, I quickly showered and grabbed a shirt that was really long on me. It looked like a dress and boxer shorts. I was wearing Kol's clothes. I sniffed them, they smelled freshly laundered. Feeling clean and satisfied, I stepped outside.

There was a seating area with a brown leather sectional. Past that, Kol was sitting on a long wooden table. The place was marble, lined with gold. It was opulent, befitting a prince. Kol had a cup in his hand, hovering in the air, forgotten as he stared at me.

I looked down and felt heat creep up my face. "Uh...thanks for letting me borrow your clothes," I said and hurriedly sat on the opposite side of him to hide my skinny legs. I bet as a prince, he didn't have many women wear his clothes. Oh god, his fiancé would be furious to find out I'd slept on his bed, and now was wearing his clothes.

But I didn't feel guilty. I actually kinda liked it.

"Will your fiancé mind that I'm here?" I glanced at him from under my lashes as I scooped eggs on my plate.

"She doesn't come here," he said.

I raised a brow.

He sighed and set his utensils down. "My parents arranged the marriage. It's not by choice. Although Carla would like the world to know we are together, we are not."

"Sounds complicated," I mumbled in between bites of toast. "So, what do we do in the meantime? I'm sure you have better use of your time than to babysit me."

"Nope. I'm perfectly fine where I'm at. It could be days before they can safely come to get you."

My eyebrows rose. "You mean, we could be stuck here for days?"

"I don't know. I'm just saying. They can't lead anyone here, so they will be careful."

I leaned back heavily. "I need to know if they're okay," I whispered.

He eyed me for a moment, then nodded his head. "I'll try to gather information for you."

"Thank you." We finished breakfast in silence. His gaze darted in my direction often, but he said nothing.

After breakfast, I paced in his spacious living room as I worried about the princes. Kol stepped in front of me and grabbed my arms gently. "Vi, they will be okay."

Once again, I was lost in his piercing green eyes until finally, I nodded. He stepped away, but I couldn't stop pacing.

"Okay. Stay here. Promise me you won't leave the suite, and I'll go gather intel for you."

"I promise." I flashed him a big, grateful smile, which he returned. My heart fluttered at the sight. Kol was beautiful, and when he smiled, it disarmed me.

I expected Kol to return shortly, but it had been over an hour. When I tired of pacing, I explored the four other rooms in the suite. They were just spare bedrooms, and one of them was locked. It surprised me he took me to his private bedroom instead of the guest bedroom. Finally, I lay in his bed and waited there. I stared at the ceiling, finding the numb state I was in soon after I lost Mom. I lost track of time and must have dozed off to sleep because I woke up to a dip on the bed, and Tristan and Sebastian's face hovered in front of me.

Was I dreaming?

No, love. It's us, Tristan said, leaning down and capturing my mouth. I pulled him close, relieved to feel him safe.

Then Sebastian pushed him off and invaded my mouth with his tongue. I kissed him with the same passion as Tristan. *I was so worried. I'm so glad you're here and safe.*

Sebastian didn't release me right away, but I sensed something he tried to hide. I pulled away.

"What is it? How's Rahl?" I asked, sitting up. I looked around the room, but Kol wasn't there.

"He's fine. He's at a secured location, commanding his army," Tristan said as he played with my hands.

"How about Mr. Wilson and Carlisle?" My hand flew to my mouth. "Oh my god. What about Shay and Lori? Are they okay?"

Sebastian took hold of my other hand. "Vi, everyone is okay. There were some student fatalities and many injuries from the Casters' attack, but it could have been worse. It helped that we expected the witches to make a move, so our people were ready. Carlisle and his coven and a few who don't support the high priestess were also ready. They protected a lot of the students. Some Vampires sided with the Casters, while many worked with the rest to drive the Casters away. They also attacked the tower. Their goal was to capture you and weaken Rahl at the same time."

"Your friends are with their pack, and Carlisle is back with his coven," Tristan said.

My face scrunched in anger. "Please tell me you captured those evil witches."

Sebastian bowed his head as he shook it sadly. "No. Unfortunately, soon after you and Kol left, their coven descended on us, but Rahl was ready with the Shifter army, so we left and went straight to the command center."

"We're sorry we couldn't get to you right away. We are being watched closely. We are officially at war with the Casters. Although they don't have the power to come at us head-to-head, they still want to take you. We couldn't risk it. With all the confusion, they didn't know that you left with Kol. They think you took off on your own while Kol and Carlisle went to their people."

"So, what do we do now? Where do we go?"

The two shared a look and gazed back at me with a pained look.

"What is it?" I asked hesitantly, not wanting to know the answer.

"Coming to you right now was risky, but we had a tight alibi. We are the envoy to the Vampire king. We needed to know which side he's on. Kol took us to you on our way out. So, the spies wouldn't know that we saw you," Sebastian said.

"I'm sorry, Vi. You have to stay here with Kol. It's safer for you. The Casters don't know where you are while they are constantly attacking us at all fronts. We can't risk it."

"I can help," I said stubbornly.

"We know you can, but this is not your fight. This is between the royals. Please trust that we can hold our own in a fight against Casters." Tristan cupped my face.

"But I can't be away from you all. Especially as you're fighting. I'll constantly worry. I couldn't reach you through our bond."

"We didn't dare try communicating that way. We were warned that powerful witches could pick up on that link and trace you that way." Sebastian grabbed a phone from his pocket and handed it to me, which I clenched tightly. "Here, it's secure. We will text you, but don't respond and don't call unless it's an emergency."

"How long do I have to stay here?" I asked.

"Until it's safe. They need to see us with Rahl, and we need to be there with our people. We're so sorry, Vi. We don't want to be away from you either, but this is the best choice. We trust Kol, and your safety is more important to us." Tristan pressed his lips gently to mine once more.

"We need to go. We don't want anyone suspecting anything," Sebastian said as he leaned down and pressed his lips on mine. "I love you, Vi."

"I love you too, Seb," I said as tears started flowing.

"You take care of yourself and don't do anything reckless. We will be together again soon," Tristan said, kissing me. "Love you," he whispered.

"Love you too," I whispered back.

They got up, and I followed them. I watched them until they disappeared through the door as silent tears fell from my face. Shortly after, Kol came back and wrapped me in his arms.

"They will be with you again soon," he whispered and kissed the top of my head.

I hugged him tightly, glad to have him on my side.

He led me to the room and stayed with me. I glanced at the phone and saw that there was a text from C. It said, *Stay put, Princess. We will see you again soon.*

I knew it was from Carlisle, which brought a smile to my face. I didn't know what connection I had with Carlisle and Kol, but I was glad to have them on my side. I could get through it as I patiently waited for my mates to be by my side again. I looked up at Kol and reached for his hand, then squeezed it with a smile.

"Thank you for everything, Kol."

"You're welcome, Princess."

NOW A COMPLETE SERIES. Get a copy to the prequel and the conclusion to the series in the next few pages.

About the Author

Https://www.facebook.com/Lina-Bengston-Author-353743682356179[1]
https://www.instagram.com/lina.bengston
https://www.subscribepage.com/lina-bengston-author

---

1. https://www.facebook.com/Lina-Bengston-Author-353743682356179

Also by Lina Bengston
Vampire Heir

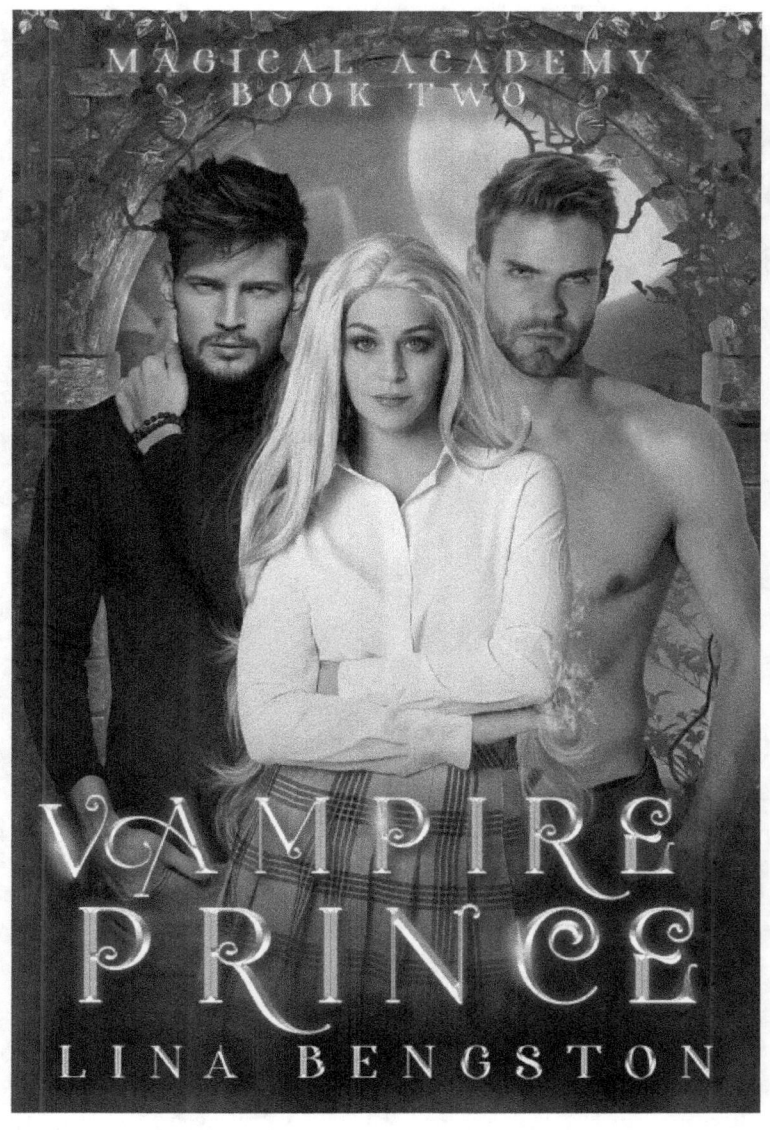

I thought the knowledge of my past would solve my problems...boy, was I wrong.

If only I could return to a time in which my life was simple. Things were less complicated in those days. Now my life is in danger, and I'm not sure what supernatural race is after me.

Luckily, I have the support of my shapeshifter heir boyfriends. But, against more powerful enemies, we need the vampire heir and the sorcerer heir on our side. However, this complicates our relationship a great deal.

The Heirs must come together soon, or we will not survive the constant attacks we face.

This is a fast burn paranormal romance where the heroine doesn't have to choose.

Violence, Foul language, and Adult content included.

Queen of Vampires

They say there's a fine line between love and hate.

Oh, no doubt about it. Just as I thought our relationship was moving toward something more. All four of my best friends dumped me at the same time—without a word of explanation. And to make things worse, they've become my tormentor for four years.

Now, I detest them passionately. However, they seem to be always around—like they've become my own personal stalkers. Regardless of what they want, I will never forgive them... Or will I?

Something big is going down. I know it in my bones, and I suspect it involves the four douches. However, the joke's on them. I'm not interested, especially if it concerns my sworn enemies.

Queen of Vampires is a standalone steamy romance where no choosing is required. The novel includes light bullying themes and adult scenes.

Viola's Birth: Magical Academy Prequel

C asters believe they should rule the supernatural race. These rebels are determined to overthrow the current monarchy.

To achieve this, they need an army. They will sacrifice innocent people to ensure they reach their goals. Nobody is safe. Not even the Shifter heir.

Just when Bea accepted her death at the hands of the Casters; a known enemy rescued her. Now she must find the strength within her to face the Vampire heir.

Will Dante end the last line of Shifters, or will he save Bea? Together, will they stop the rebellion or pave the way to provide the Casters the weapon they had been pursuing—a hybrid warrior.

This prequel is a tragic story about Vi's creation.

This novella is not RH.

Violence, Foul language, and Adult content included.

Trigger Warning: Please read the details at the front of the book.

Don't miss out!

Visit the website below and you can sign up to receive emails whenever Lina Bengston publishes a new book. There's no charge and no obligation.

https://books2read.com/r/B-A-MMVM-IYMKB

BOOKS 2 READ

Connecting independent readers to independent writers.

Also by Lina Bengston

Her Protectors
Queen of Vampires

Magical Academy
King's Heirs